Praise

MIMI

A Holiday By Gaslight

"Readers will easily fall for Sophie and Ned in their gaslit surroundings."

-*Library Journal, starred review*

"Matthews' novella is full of comfort and joy—a sweet treat for romance readers that's just in time for Christmas."

-*Kirkus Reviews*

"A graceful love story...and an authentic presentation of the 1860s that reads with the simplicity and visual gusto of a period movie."

-*Readers' Favorite*

The Matrimonial Advertisement

"For this impressive Victorian romance, Matthews (*The Viscount and the Vicar's Daughter*) crafts a tale that sparkles with chemistry and impresses with strong character development... an excellent series launch..."

-*Publishers Weekly*

"Matthews (*The Viscount and the Vicar's Daughter*) has a knack for creating slow-building chemistry and an intriguing plot with a social history twist."

-*Library Journal*

"Matthews' (*The Pug Who Bit Napoleon*, 2018, etc.) series opener is a guilty pleasure, brimming with beautiful people, damsels in distress, and an abundance of testosterone...A well-written and engaging story that's more than just a romance."

-Kirkus Reviews

The Viscount and the Vicar's Daughter

"Matthews' tale hits all the high notes of a great romance novel... Cue the satisfied sighs of romance readers everywhere."

-Kirkus Reviews

"Matthews pens a heartfelt romance that culminates into a sweet ending that will leave readers happy. A wonderfully romantic read."

-RT Book Reviews

The Lost Letter

"The perfect quick read for fans of Regency romances as well as Victorian happily-ever-afters, with shades of Austen and the Brontës that create an entertaining blend of drama and romance."

-RT Book Reviews

"A fast and emotionally satisfying read, with two characters finding the happily-ever-after they had understandably given up on. A promising debut."

-Library Journal

A HOLIDAY BY GASLIGHT

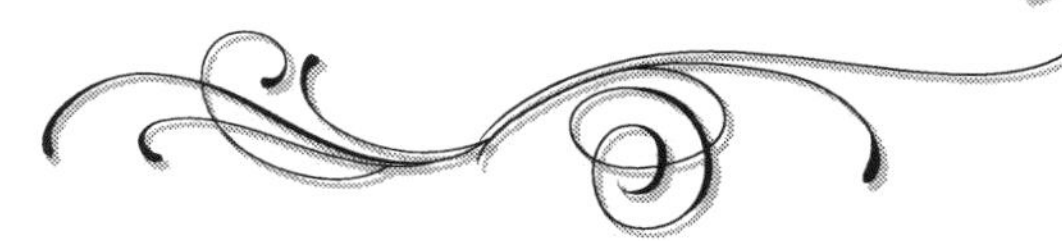

A VICTORIAN CHRISTMAS NOVELLA

MIMI MATTHEWS

A HOLIDAY BY GASLIGHT
A Victorian Christmas Novella

Edited by Deborah Nemeth
Cover Design by James T. Egan of Bookfly Design
Interior Design & Typesetting by Ampersand Book Interiors

E-Book: 978-0-9990364-6-4
Paperback: 978-0-9990364-7-1

WWW.PERFECTLYPROPERPRESS.COM

In memory of Christmas Marzipan
"Zippy"
2008-2018

ONE

London, England
November, 1861

An icy late November breeze rustled the bare branches of the trees along the Serpentine. Hyde Park was practically deserted at this time of morning. And no wonder. It was freezing cold, the gray skies heavy with the scent of impending rain. Sophie Appersett thrust her hands more firmly into the confines of the oversized mink muff she wore suspended from a silken cord round her neck. "So you see, Mr. Sharpe. There's no reason to continue as we are."

Edward Sharpe walked at her side in complete silence. His large gloved hands were clasped behind his back, his deep blue eyes fixed straight ahead. His expression was somber. So somber that, when paired with his severe black suit, black topcoat, and black beaver hat, he might easily have been mistaken for a man on his way to a funeral.

No one who saw him now would ever believe he was one of the wealthiest manufactory owners in Greater London. And they certainly wouldn't credit him as being part owner of not one but two separate railway concerns.

Sophie cast him a sidelong glance. He was a handsome man, if one liked tall, dark males of the serious variety, but he was infuriatingly difficult to read. He never betrayed his feelings with a look or a word. And when it came to conversation, silence was, by far, his favorite subject. During their brief courtship, she'd been obliged to do most of the talking.

In the past two months, she'd come to hate the sound of her own voice. It was always droning on and on, filling up the vast emptiness between them with magpie-like chatter. Forever talking, talking, talking, but never really *saying* anything.

But she was saying something now. Something she should have said two months ago. "We simply do not suit."

"No indeed, ma'am." Mr. Sharpe's voice was a deep, rich baritone. He had no discernible accent. Quite the opposite. He spoke in the cultured tones of a gentleman. Where he'd learned to do so, she hadn't the slightest idea. His parents were London shopkeepers. He'd never gone to Eton or Cambridge. Instead, he'd spent his youth delivering packages and stocking the shelves of their store.

And now he was one and thirty. Wealthy, powerful, and—according to her parents—imminently eligible.

"*He's trying to gain entrée into polite society,*" Mama had said when she and Papa first broached the subject of an alliance. "*It's why he wants to court you, my dear.*"

"*And he'll never flaunt his common origins in your face,*" Papa had added. "*He's too ashamed of them. Now he's made his fortune, he wishes to forget his humble beginnings. And if he can forget them, Sophia, then so can you.*"

Sophie didn't care about Mr. Sharpe's humble beginnings. Quite the opposite. She'd often wished he would speak of them. She'd been curious about him and desired to know him better. But after two months...

She sighed. "I haven't told my parents yet. I know they'll be dreadfully disappointed. They like you very much."

"I expect they do," he said.

She shot him a narrow glance. His face was set in lines as immoveable as granite, his broad shoulders taut beneath the expensive fabric of his topcoat. "You needn't be unpleasant about it. They were no more mercenary than you."

"Mercenary," he repeated. "Is that what I've been?"

"It's nothing to be ashamed of. It's how these things are done. It's how they've always been done. Alliances contrived between wealthy merchant's daughters and impoverished nobleman. Or—as in our situation—successful men of business and the daughters of impoverished country gentry." A troubled frown clouded her brow. "I'm sorry it's all come to nothing for you."

"Are you?"

"Yes, but...honestly, Mr. Sharpe, if you wish to gain admittance into society, you would do better to look higher than the Appersetts of Derbyshire. Find yourself an earl's daughter. A lady who is accustomed to moving about in society. As for myself, I—"

"Is there someone else?" he asked abruptly.

Sophie's gaze jerked to his. "What?"

"Is there another man? Someone you prefer?"

"Goodness no. If there were, I'd never have agreed to walk out with you." She slowed her pace. They'd ventured too far from the entrance to the park. And she couldn't stay much longer. She had to get back before her absence was remarked.

"It's only that we have nothing at all in common. After two months, surely you must see that."

He made no reply.

Sophie worried her lower lip between her teeth. How much more was she required to say in order to put an end to their relationship? She had no experience with this sort of thing. No man had ever asked leave to court her before. And, she thought grimly, it was very possible that no man ever would again. "Perhaps I should have said something sooner."

"Why didn't you?"

She looked out across the choppy waters of the Serpentine. "I don't know. I suppose I thought..." That he would warm to her. That he would come to care for her. Even to love her a little. She'd been ready to love him. It would have taken so little encouragement. A fond glance. A kind word. An affectionate touch. "But it doesn't matter now, does it? We've come to the natural end of things."

"As you say." Mr. Sharpe withdrew his gold pocket watch from his waistcoat to look at the time. It was a singularly dismissive gesture.

Sophie stopped. The chill breeze rustled her heavy woolen skirts around her legs. "Am I keeping you from an appointment, sir?"

He stopped as well, turning to face her. His expression remained unreadable, but she detected a slight hardening along the firm line of his jaw. As if he were irritated—or even angry. "You are, Miss Appersett."

An embarrassed flush crept into her cheeks. Here she was attempting to sever their relationship in the most delicate manner possible, and all he could think about was his next meeting! He didn't even care. The past two months had been as nothing to him. It was what she'd always suspected, but still…

It hurt. She had so wanted him to like her.

She clenched her fingers within the confines of her muff. "I will not detain you. If all is settled between us—"

"Yes, yes," he said impatiently. "We don't suit."

"Then you agree—"

"Perfectly. There's no reason to continue this charade."

Sophie inwardly winced. A charade? Is that what he thought of their courtship? How utterly lowering. "No reason at all." She withdrew her hand from her muff and extended it to him. "I wish you well, Mr. Sharpe."

Mr. Sharpe's gaze dropped to her outstretched hand. It was encased in a red kid glove, slightly worn at the thumb. After a moment of hesitation, his much larger hand engulfed hers, clasping it just a heartbeat longer than was strictly necessary. "And I you, Miss Appersett," he said.

And then he let her go.

Ned threw his hat and gloves onto the upholstered settee in his office with such force that his tall beaver hat ricocheted against the cushions and onto the floor. He didn't pick it up. Instead, he raked both hands through his hair until it stood half on end. He had a cowlick near his forehead, an infuriating feature which made his thick black locks impossible to tame. Even a liberal application of Macassar oil couldn't civilize them for long.

Well, there was no more point in civilizing his hair, nor in civilizing himself. Miss Appersett was gone from his life.

Their courtship was over. And any hopes of something more were at an end.

After a long moment, he shrugged off his topcoat and tossed it over a chair. His frock coat followed. He rolled up his shirtsleeves as he made his way to the enormous mahogany barrister's desk by the window. Stacks of carefully organized papers covered the surface, a marble paperweight securing the financial statements he'd been perusing when Miss Appersett's note had arrived. The note itself was folded inside an inner pocket of his coat, the scrawled words emblazoned on his brain.

Dear Mr. Sharpe,

Will you do me the courtesy of meeting me at the entrance to Hyde Park at 10 o'clock? There is something of importance I need to discuss with you.

Sincerely,
S.A.

God knows what he'd expected to happen. This entire affair had been the equivalent of walking blindfolded along a cliff's edge. The only way he'd managed to navigate was by going at a snail's pace. Even then, he'd often hemmed and halted and hesitated—never knowing when he might put a foot wrong and plummet straight down over the side.

Courtship among the upper classes was a delicate business governed by more rules than a Chancery suit. He'd been completely out of his depth, forced to rely on the rather vague advice administered in the *Gentlemen's Book of Etiquette*.

Rule No. 1: When you see a lady who impresses you favorably, do not be in any rash haste to make advances.

"What bollocks," he muttered.

It would have been so much easier if Miss Appersett had asked him for money or a gift of some sort. He'd have happily given her anything she wanted. He'd already spent a small fortune on her engagement ring. It was a flawless brilliant-cut diamond, presently residing in the bottommost drawer of his desk. He'd intended to give it to her next month. Her parents had invited him to their Derbyshire estate for the Christmas holiday. Sir William and Lady Appersett had made no secret that they expected him to propose marriage to their daughter during his stay.

Not that he'd felt obligated in any way. If he'd wanted to put an end to his relationship with Miss Appersett, he'd have done so without hesitation. But he hadn't wanted to end things. He'd been besotted with Sophia Appersett since almost the first moment he laid eyes on her.

It had been mid-June at the opening of the new Horticultural Gardens at South Kensington. Prince Albert himself had been presiding over the occasion. Ned saw Miss Appersett standing with another lady on the terrace at the top of the arcade. He passed behind them along the rock asphalt promenade.

"Mr. Sharpe! Is that you?"

He stopped to respond, recognizing the lady as the wife of Vincent Carstairs, heir to the Carstairs shipping fortune. Vincent was a casual acquaintance of his. A man who, like Ned, was not strictly a gentleman, but had earned a measure of acceptance in polite society by virtue of his good looks, good manners, and sizeable bank balance. And, of course, it didn't hurt that Vincent had managed to marry the daughter of a viscount.

Ned greeted her with civility, if not warmth. "Mrs. Carstairs."

She motioned to her companion. "Allow me to introduce my friend, Miss Sophia Appersett."

Miss Appersett turned, looking at him with a slight smile.

And Ned was struck dumb. There was no other way to describe it. The sight of Miss Appersett, with her creamy porcelain skin, lustrous sable hair, and wide, melting brown eyes, rendered him speechless. Quickened his pulse and temporarily fogged his brain.

She was a beautiful girl, possessed of an elegant bearing and a sweet expression. A classic English rose. Indeed, her perfect oval face might well have been set on a cameo. But the spark of sharp intelligence in the soft velvet of her gaze and the stubborn set to her dimpled chin spoke of a female who was much more than the sum of her face and her figure.

"Mr. Sharpe," she said, extending her hand.

He scarcely had the presence of mind to take it. He just stood there and stared at her like a great, uncultured lummox. As if he'd never before encountered a lady.

"Miss Appersett is the daughter of Sir William of Appersett House in Derbyshire," Mrs. Carstairs said. "Surely you've heard of Appersett House?"

Indeed Ned had. A fact that made his course of action all the clearer.

Sophia Appersett was a baronet's daughter. A member of polite society whose family boasted a bloodline that could be traced back to the court of Henry VIII. What better lady with whom to align his fortunes?

He was all of one and thirty and had been contemplating marriage for the past year at least. But he'd never actually wanted to marry until he laid eyes on Miss Appersett. Within ten minutes of meeting her, he'd pictured her on his arm as he attended the entertainments of the season. Within a month, he'd envisioned her presiding over his house and warming his bed. His wife. Mrs. Sophia Sharpe, daughter of Sir William of Appersett House.

Setting his plan in motion had taken no effort at all. Sir William was practically a bankrupt. His only asset, besides his famous estate in Derbyshire, was the vast beauty possessed by his two daughters. He and his wife had brought Miss Appersett and her younger sister, Emily, to London with the hopes of finding them rich husbands.

And Ned *was* rich, for all the good it had done him.

He sat down behind his desk and resumed reading his reports. He might as well have attempted to read a document written in ancient Greek. He couldn't focus. Couldn't rid his mind of the sound of Miss Appersett's quiet voice uttering those five fateful words.

We simply do not suit.

A sharp rap at the door wrenched Ned from his melancholy thoughts. He looked up to see his business partner, Walter Murray, strolling into his office.

"Well?" Walter asked.

Ned cast aside his papers and met his friend's inquiring eyes. "I've been jilted."

"*What?*"

"You heard me."

Walter sat in the chair across from him as Ned apprised him of his meeting with Miss Appersett. When he finished,

Walter gave an eloquent grimace. "You have my sympathies. But...she's not entirely wrong about the two of you being ill-suited."

Ned scowled. "What's that supposed to mean?"

"You're as different as chalk and cheese."

"How the devil would you know?"

"I've seen you together. That afternoon at Cremorne Gardens when we watched the high-wire act. And then again at Mrs. Ashburnham's dinner party. I had more in common with Miss Appersett's little sister than you had with Miss Appersett herself."

"Rubbish."

"You hardly said two words to the girl."

"Not all of us are blessed with your innate charm."

Walter snorted. "It wasn't lack of charm. Though I won't disagree that you fall short in that department. It was that you never seemed yourself around her—as if you were trying to be someone else."

"I was trying to be respectful. To abide by the rules."

"It's not the way you would have courted a mason's daughter."

Ned glared at his friend. Walter was himself the son of a stonemason. The two of them had grown up together, both ambitious and both anxious to gain acceptance into society. "Miss Appersett isn't a mason's daughter. Her father only gave me leave to court her because I have money. Because he believed I could pass for one of them."

"Just because you can pass for one of them doesn't mean you are one of them."

"A brilliant observation."

"It's the truth. Sometimes I think you forget it."

"I *never* forget it," Ned said in a low voice. The assertion betrayed far more feeling than he'd intended.

Walter's expression briefly softened. "You're truly broken up about this, aren't you?"

Was he? Ned didn't know. In all honesty, he couldn't tell what he was feeling at the moment. A bewildering mass of disappointment, anger, and heartache was churning in his chest and in his stomach. He was quite tempted to put his fist through the wall. Either that or retire to his rooms with a large bottle of whiskey. Perhaps he was coming down with something?

"Did you love her?" Walter asked.

"No." It was the truth. He hadn't loved Sophia Appersett. How could he? He hardly knew her. Their relationship had never progressed beyond the veriest commonplace discussions about current events or the weather. Even then, Miss Appersett had done most of the talking.

And yet, seeing her had been the brightest spot in his day.

No, it hadn't been love, but it had been...something. Something warm and filled with promise. Something that was gone now, irrevocably, leaving him empty and alone.

"I admired her. A great deal."

The understatement of a lifetime.

"And Miss Appersett didn't admire you in return, is that it?" Walter considered the matter. "What does that etiquette book of yours advise in these circumstances? A tin of sweets? A flowery apology?"

Ned stifled a groan. "I wish to God I'd never told you about that blasted book."

Walter flashed a broad grin. It only served to make Ned more irritable. Things had always been easy for Walter Murray.

He had a natural way about him. A twinkle in his green eyes and a spring in his step. With his long, lean frame and ginger-colored hair, he wasn't particularly handsome. Nevertheless, people seemed to like him. *Women* seemed to like him.

"What you should do," he advised, "is wait until Christmas and then, when you're in Derbyshire, fall on your knees and beg her for a second chance."

Ned leaned forward, resting his head in his hands. He was beginning to develop a pounding headache.

There would be no second chance with Miss Appersett. And even if there were, what use would it be? She'd already rejected him at his gentlemanly best. He had nothing left to offer her. No further way to prove himself worthy.

"I won't be going to Derbyshire for Christmas."

"Why not?"

"Damnation, Walter. Haven't you heard a word I've been saying? My relationship with Miss Appersett is over. She's called it off."

"Ah, but has she rescinded your invitation to Appersett House?"

Ned gave a short, humorless laugh. "No, but I'm not likely to go, am I? Not after Miss Appersett's given me my marching orders."

"But—"

"She's made her feelings plain and I mean to respect them."

"And that's an end to it?"

"It is." Ned returned his attention to his papers, resolved to ignore the heavy ache in his heart. "My time with Miss Appersett was a pleasant interlude, but now it's over. I shall go on as I did before. The world doesn't end simply because I've had a personal disappointment."

But he certainly felt like it had.

TWO

"Y*ou told him what?"*

Sophie winced at the outrage in her father's voice. She'd known he'd be upset by her news, but she hadn't anticipated he'd lose his temper to quite such a degree. "It's really for the best, Papa. If you'd but consider—"

"You foolish, empty-headed girl. Have you any idea what you've done?" Papa advanced upon her, his round, fleshy face red as a beetroot. "You had no business speaking to the man. No business at all—"

"Mind your temper, my dear," her mother warned. She was seated on the overstuffed drawing room sofa, a scrap of needlework in her hand. With her elegantly inclined head and impeccable posture, she looked almost queenly. One hardly noticed that her black taffeta day dress was out of date—the color a little faded and the well-worn hem turned and mended within an inch of its life.

"I have not lost my temper," Papa said. "But when I think of all our plans—the expenses here in London—the lease on this infernal townhouse—all so you and your ungrateful sister might—"

"What have I to do with it?" Emily cried out from her place near the fire. She was still finishing her tea, a honey-slathered scone suspended halfway to her mouth. A drop of honey threatened to plop down onto her skirts.

Sophie leaned forward in alarm. "Emmy, do be careful!"

Unlike Mama's old taffeta, Emily's dress was new. It was a delicate pink-and-yellow floral confection made only last week by a fashionable modiste in Bond Street. Removing a stain would be well-nigh impossible without fading the print.

"Don't be such a fusspot." Emily caught the drop of honey on her finger a fraction of a second before it fell, then popped her finger into her mouth.

Mama sighed. "Emily, use your napkin, do."

Papa continued to pace, his face getting redder by the minute. "Is it too much to ask that my daughters do their part? That they for once—just for once—show a degree of gratitude for all the sacrifices I've made for them?"

Sophie shot her mother a desperate glance. When Papa was in such a state, no one else could bring him to his senses.

Mama lay aside her needlework and rose from the sofa. With characteristic languor, she strolled to the drinks table and poured out a large measure of brandy. "Come, my love." She pressed the half-filled glass into Papa's hand. "If you succumb to a fit of apoplexy, you'll be of no use to anyone."

"These ungrateful girls," Papa muttered as he raised the glass to his lips. "They do you no credit, madam."

Emily gave another indignant huff. "I haven't done anything wrong. I don't see why I must be scolded simply because Sophie has—"

"Hush," Mama said. She turned to Sophie. "Come, dear. Let's have a walk in the garden, shall we? I could do with an airing."

Sophie's spirits sank. She could withstand Papa's remonstrations. It didn't matter how much he bellowed or threatened. But Mama applied an altogether different—and far more effective—technique.

She linked her slim arm through Sophie's as they exited the drawing room. "Is it damp out? Will we need our coats?"

"No, Mama. Just a shawl, I think."

The townhouse on Green Street was small but elegant. It had a neat little back garden with trees and shrubs laid out in a welcoming design. In the summer it was filled with the scent of fresh greenery and fragrant blooms. Now it was as stark and bare as the landscape along the Serpentine.

Her mother led her down a barren path at the edge of the garden. They walked in silence for several minutes. And then, "You must forgive your father," she said.

Sophie felt a twinge of bitterness at the unfairness of it all. It didn't last long. It never did. "There's nothing to forgive. I know I've disappointed him. I wish it were otherwise." She paused before adding, "But I won't let him bully me into marrying a gentleman I don't like."

"Bully you? He would never do any such thing. Nor would I. We only want what's best for you and your sister. Surely, you know that?" She squeezed Sophie's arm. "Besides, I wasn't aware you disliked Mr. Sharpe."

"I don't dislike him. Not really."

"But you object to him? You never said so. What's changed, my love? Has he done something? Said something?"

"He's done nothing. *Said* nothing." Sophie stopped on the garden path to face her mother. "We have nothing in common, Mama. Not a single blessed thing. And I know he must feel the awkwardness of it as keenly as I do. Indeed, when I told him I wished to put an end to our courtship, he seemed almost...relieved."

"Did he? Well, then I daresay you've done the right thing." She once again linked her arm through Sophie's. "Come. Let's walk. It's too cold to be standing still. You'll get a chill on your lungs and we can't have that. Not so close to Christmas."

They continued in the direction of the mews. The rattle of carriage wheels and the clip-clop of horses' hooves sounded in the distance. There was a black iron gate at the end of the garden, a convenient shortcut to the stables and, thereby, to the street. It was how Sophie had slipped away to meet Mr. Sharpe in Hyde Park.

That had been only a few days ago. Three and half days, to be precise. It had taken her that long to muster up the courage to tell her parents what she'd done. Which was unlike her, now she thought of it. Usually, when she made an independent decision, she had the confidence to reveal it to her family without delay. This time, however, she hadn't felt very confident. Indeed, it wasn't long after leaving Hyde Parke that she'd begun to experience a niggling sensation of doubt.

"What do you suppose Mr. Darwin would make of your decision?" Mama asked.

Sophie wrapped her shawl more tightly about her shoulders. "I don't see that Mr. Darwin has much to do with my present situation."

"Doesn't his book advise altering one's behavior? Adapting oneself to changing circumstances in order to ensure survival?"

"He was speaking in terms of evolutionary theory, not issuing practical advice for young ladies."

"As I recall, it was you who claimed such theories could apply to our modern society. Or was that just a means of convincing yourself to accept Mr. Sharpe's suit?"

Sophie couldn't remember exactly what she'd said. She was new to reading Mr. Darwin's works and his latest, *On the Origin of Species*, was still very much a mystery to her. "I believe one must accept the modern world," she said carefully. "Even if it makes one uncomfortable to do so. We none of us can avoid progress. We must change ourselves constantly in order to grow with the times. Either that or risk being left behind. But there are limits, Mama."

"And you've reached yours with Mr. Sharpe?"

"I have. And let that be an end to it." She was done with reviewing the pathetic business of her failed romance. She'd made a decision—a sensible one, at that—and she had a mind to stick to it, no matter the consequences.

And there would be consequences. There always were when she butted heads with her father. But she absolutely refused to let the prospect dampen her holiday spirits. The weeks leading up to Christmas were her favorite of the year.

She inhaled a breath of crisp morning air "If only Papa wasn't so angry with me."

Mama made a soft chuffing sound. "He's not angry. He's worried."

"About money?"

Her mother gave a reluctant nod. She didn't like discussing their finances, but she and Sophie had an understanding of sorts when it came to matters of money. An unspoken acknowledgment that they would share the burden of Papa and Emily's excess.

"We've spent a great deal too much on our stay in London," she said. "He'd hoped you and Emily would make a success of it. If you had, it would've all been worth it. As it is, we shall have to give up our lease and return to Derbyshire. Which is too bad, really. There are no suitable gentlemen there for Emily. Only this morning Lady Colson recommended we give her another season. If you were married—and married well—we could bring her out as we should. No more skimping on little luxuries."

Sophie steeled herself against her mother's words. She refused to be made to feel guilty.

Mama gave Sophie's arm another squeeze. "You're not to think we value Emily's happiness more than yours, my dear. But you must allow that your sister is not as sensible as we are. She's more like your father."

"She's selfish."

"And you, my pet, are too severe."

"Am I? It seems I've spent my life making sacrifices for Emily's comfort—and for Papa's—because I'm sensible and know my duty to the family. Is it so unforgiveable that I should wish to marry someone I might like just a little, and who might like me in return for reasons other than my pedigree? I don't require love. I'm not so silly as that. But you ask me to leave our family, to marry a stranger and live out the rest of my days in his house, as his possession. That isn't the same as dying my old gowns and thrice-darning my stockings so that Emily might wear the latest fashions."

Her mother frowned. "No, indeed. We've asked a great deal of you, haven't we? It hasn't always been fair."

"I've never complained."

"I wouldn't blame you if you had. Your sister and your father have a taste for fine things. They aren't always wise. While you and I… Well, we love our family, don't we? We aspire to do what's best for them. And if such can be achieved by a small sacrifice here and there—"

"A *small* sacrifice? Really, Mama."

"Wearing last season's dresses or eating beef only once a week, I meant. Not marriage."

Sophie cast a glance at her mother. Three years before, when Papa had first begun the repairs and modernizations to Appersett House, she'd appeared to support his decision. And later, when the household budget had been reduced to practically nothing, she'd contrived various ways to make do.

The economizing had grated, especially on Emily.

"*What use is a gaslit ballroom if we cannot entertain?*" she regularly complained.

But much as it bothered Emily—and even Papa, on occasion—Sophie had never thought it bothered her mother a great deal. Indeed, Mama had seemed to consider their reduced circumstances a challenge to her cleverness.

Had she merely been putting on a cheerful face?

A knot formed in Sophie's stomach as she registered the fine lines of worry between her mother's brows and the faint shadows beneath her eyes. Their circumstances must be precarious indeed if Mama was losing sleep over them.

"No," Mama said. "Marriage—especially to a gentleman of Mr. Sharpe's ilk—is no small sacrifice. Your father and I were wrong to ask it of you. The poor fellow would have never fit in with our sort of people. He's a bit coarse, isn't he?"

"I never thought him so."

"And rather too stern about the mouth."

"He's a serious man, certainly, but—"

"These quiet, brooding types sometimes conceal a fearsome temper. Who knows how ill he may have treated you if given half a chance?"

"Mr. Sharpe is not an ogre, Mama."

"All the same. I see why you'd wish to avoid the match."

Sophie was silent. She had the distinct impression that her mother was managing her. A frustrating—and all-too-common—experience.

"I shall explain it all to your father when he's calmed down a bit," Mama continued. "And then we shall go home. I confess, it will be a relief."

"I'm sorry," Sophie said. "I did try to make it work. Had I known—"

"Naturally, my love. I don't fault you. I only wish we hadn't suffered the expense of staying in London. And then there's the Christmas party to think of. Another dreadful expense."

"Is it too late to cancel it?"

"And disappoint your father? I daren't suggest such a thing. He's so dreadfully proud of how well the house looks. This will be his first chance to properly show it off."

"But—"

"No. You must trust me on this matter. A Christmas celebration won't send us to debtor's prison. And it will make your father and sister so very happy. As for the rest of it… well." She gave a heavy sigh, sounding suddenly more tired that Sophie had ever heard before. "We shall think of that in the new year."

THREE

"Sharpe and Murray," Emily read aloud from the sign over the door. "Rather like Scrooge and Marley, isn't it?"

"Hush, Emmy." Sophie was in no mood for her sister's little jokes, even if Mr. Sharpe's office in Fleet Street did put her in mind of something out of one of Mr. Dickens' novels. It was dark and unwelcoming—and situated far too close to the river for her comfort. Not the sort of place two young ladies should be visiting so near to dusk, even if they did have a maidservant in tow.

"Oh, miss," Annie said, her voice pleading. "We shouldn't be here."

"I agree with Annie," Emily said. "This was a fool's errand. No one's at home. There are no lamps lit in the windows. And the street is empty."

"It's not his residence. It's his office." Sophie reached up to ring the bell. "You may wait in the carriage if you like."

Emily's expression turned mulish. "I'd like to go back to Green Street."

Sophie could have happily throttled her sister. She had no use for her dramatics, least of all on such a delicate errand as this. She'd wanted Annie to accompany her alone, but Emily had insisted on joining them, and once Emily set her mind to something there was no dissuading her.

"I want to go back *now*," Emily said.

"Then go." Sophie gave the bell a determined tug.

"And leave you here? How will you get back? It's too far to walk."

"I'll hail a hackney."

Emily looked out at the empty street. There was no sign of a hackney, nor of any other conveyance for hire. "I don't like this."

"Oh, do stop going on," Sophie said, exasperated. "It's Mr. Sharpe's office, for heaven's sake, not a den of waterfront thieves. If I can't find a carriage, I daresay he'll see me home himself."

Annie stood wide-eyed next to Emily. The young maid had a perpetual expression of pale-faced terror. As if she'd just seen a ghost. Or, far worse, as if she were one step away from being cast off without a reference. "Miss? If Lady Appersett were to find out—"

"Quite," Emily said. "I'm going home. I should never have agreed to come. The risk to my reputation—"

"Yes, yes," Sophie interrupted. "Go if you must. You need say no more."

Emily nodded once. "If Mama asks, I shall tell her you're visiting Lady Dawlish."

The tightness in Sophie's chest eased a little. Emily was spoiled and selfish, it was true, but she could be rather a good sport on occasion. "See that my sister goes straight home, Annie. No stopping at the shops."

"Yes, miss." Annie hesitated only a moment before following Emily down the steps and back into the carriage.

The coachman gave the horses the office to start and the carriage set off down Fleet Street. Sophie watched it until it disappeared from sight.

And then she rang the bell again.

Visiting a gentleman's place of business—especially when that gentleman was not related by blood or marriage—was the height of impropriety. The less time she spent lingering on the front steps the better.

She tucked her hands into her muff and waited.

And waited.

At last, the sound of footsteps thumping down the stairs could be heard. The front door rattled as someone disengaged the locks at top, bottom, and center. Sophie's heart thumped high in her chest, making a creditable effort to leap into her throat. She swallowed hard as the door was flung open, revealing an irritated-looking man with a shock of carroty hair.

It was Mr. Murray, Mr. Sharpe's business partner and friend. She'd met him several times before, though never under such dubious circumstances as this.

"Miss Appersett!" he exclaimed. "What on earth are you doing here?"

"Good day to you, Mr. Murray. I've come to see, Mr. Sharpe. Is he here?"

"Er...yes. But I don't think—"

"May I come in?"

"That may not be the wisest—" Mr. Murray broke off, appearing to collect himself. "Forgive me. Yes. Do come in, ma'am." He opened the door wide and took a step back for her to enter, then shut and bolted it behind her. "Is Mr. Sharpe expecting you? He hasn't mentioned—"

"I'm not expected."

"And you've, er, come here alone?"

"I brought my sister—"

"Your sister!"

"And my maid, but they've both abandoned me, as you see." Sophie strived to sound as if she had the matter well in hand. "I saw no reason to insist they stay. The street is deserted. My presence can hardly have been remarked."

Mr. Murray's mouth quirked briefly. "My dear Miss Appersett, I've no doubt curtains have been twitching up and down Fleet Street from the moment of your arrival."

Sophie suppressed a grimace. This visit—she was beginning to realize—was not one of her better ideas. Quite the reverse, in fact.

Mr. Murray seemed sympathetic. "Come. I'd best take you to Sharpe." He gestured for her to precede him up the stairs. The rickety steps creaked under her booted feet. She caught up her heavy skirts in her hands as she climbed, mindful not to crease the fabric.

She'd dressed carefully for this visit, choosing to wear one of her most elegant afternoon gowns. Only two seasons old, it was made of rich claret-colored silk trimmed in embossed velvet ribbon. It was ridiculously flattering to her complexion and figure.

And it was as ill-suited to the premises of Sharpe and Murray as a wire crinoline was to a lightning storm.

She supposed she should feel rather silly to have put so much effort into her appearance. Then again, a lady must always don her strongest armor when going into battle.

"Forgive the state of things," Mr. Murray said. "Our clerk doesn't come in on Wednesdays."

An image of Mr. Cratchit, hunched over a tiny desk, entering figures in a ledger by the light of a guttering tallow candle, sprung fully formed into Sophie's mind.

Drat Emily for ever mentioning Scrooge and Marley!

Mr. Murray led her through another door. It opened into a sort of sitting room, equipped with a round table, wooden chairs, and a small stuffed settee positioned in front of a coal fire. There was an open door to the left of it and a closed door to the right. Offices presumably. One of them belonging to Mr. Sharpe.

"If you'll wait a moment," Mr. Murray said, "I'll tell him that you're here."

Sophie clasped her hands tightly together inside her muff. Doubts, heretofore kept at bay, now assailed her. They were as painfully overwhelming as a sudden shower of hailstones.

What on earth had possessed her to call on him in this manner? Was it temporary madness of some kind? Or merely desperation? Both, she suspected. Why else would she have embarked on a course of action so careless? So stupid? So unutterably pathetic?

Mr. Darwin said that a grain in the balance could determine the survival of an organic being. That adaptations in however slight a degree could, ultimately, shift the scales.

She privately wished Mr. Darwin to Hades.

Evolution was all well and good for organic beings, but for a young lady, alteration of one's behavior simply engendered too much risk.

What if Mr. Sharpe had been telling the truth? What if he really had found their relationship a tiresome charade? The very notion sapped her courage. She did her best to martial it. To focus on the reasons she'd come. If there was a chance she'd been wrong about him—a small possibility that, under different circumstances, they might be friends—surely it was worth the risk to her pride and reputation to find out?

Wasn't it?

Wasn't it?

But there was no turning back now.

Mr. Murray ducked his head in the office door and exchanged a few murmured words with the person within.

And then Mr. Sharpe was there, his tall, broad-shouldered frame filling the doorway. He fixed her with a cool blue stare, every inch of him more imposing—more unsettlingly masculine—than she remembered.

"Miss Appersett," he said.

"Mr. Sharpe. Good afternoon."

He looked at her for several weighted seconds, as if she were some dangerous creature escaped from the Zoological Gardens, and then he moved aside, motioning for her to join him in his office.

Her skirts brushed against his legs as she passed him. The faint scent of lemon verbena tickled her nose. It was his shaving soap. Either that or the fragrance of his pomade. She'd never been able to tell which. It mingled with the smells of his office: fresh ink and parchment and smoke from the fire.

He shut the door behind her with a decisive click. "Will you sit down?"

"Yes. Thank you." She didn't feel much like sitting, but had little choice. If she stood, he'd be bound to remain standing as well. Such were the rules of polite society and, up to this point, Mr. Sharpe had followed them to the letter.

She sank into one of the upholstered chairs opposite his desk, her skirts settling around her in a formidable spill of silk and velvet. His desk was a great wooden affair, well-suited to a gentleman of Mr. Sharpe's proportions. A barrister's desk stacked high with papers and topped with a triple inkwell, a blotter, and an oil lamp with a fluted glass shade.

When Mr. Sharpe resumed his seat behind it, she felt all at once the weakness—the absolute insignificance—of her position. Was this how a person felt when they were petitioning him for a loan or some other favor of business?

She reminded herself that she was doing neither. She required no money from him and she wanted no favors. She was simply clarifying her position, awkward as that may be. "Mr. Sharpe. Forgive me for intruding, but—"

"I hadn't thought to see you again," he said abruptly.

A frisson of anxiety rippled through her veins. His voice was colder than she'd ever heard it. Cold and taut with control. She moistened her lips. "Nor I you."

It had been a week since she'd parted ways with him. A week since she'd told him, so emphatically, that they did not suit.

"And yet…here you are." His gaze drifted over her face. Cool. Detached. As if he were taking a dispassionate inventory of all of her flaws. "Why *are* you here, Miss Appersett?"

She untied her bonnet strings. "To speak with you, obviously."

Mr. Sharpe regarded her from beneath lowered brows as she slowly removed her bonnet, her muff, and her gloves. "I haven't much time to spare you, ma'am. I have a dinner engagement at six."

"Do you?" Sophie placed her belongings on the empty chair beside her, unable to conceal a flash of chagrin. Who in the world dined at six?

"*Promptly* at six," he said.

"Hmm." She believed him, but only just. "It seems that, when it comes to you, I have uniformly bad timing."

"I can't imagine this will take long."

Well, that certainly told her. He expected her to be quick and to the point. Not only did he have better things to do, he had more important people to do them with. More important than her, anyway.

"You're not making this easy, Mr. Sharpe."

"And what is *this*, Miss Appersett? Apart from being entirely irregular."

Sophie frowned. She'd long desired him to show some emotion, but this wasn't what she'd had in mind. "I beg your pardon, sir. Are you angry with me?"

His expression hardened at the very suggestion. "You've taken me by surprise, ma'am. And you've put me in a devil of a position."

"My apologies. I didn't realize—"

"Didn't you?"

"I believed I was being discreet."

"On Fleet Street? In broad daylight?"

Sophie privately conceded his point. Perhaps she should have worn a veil? She'd considered it, naturally, but when standing in front of the pier glass in her bedroom, it had seemed altogether too dramatic a choice. She hadn't wanted to look like she was engaging in some pantomime of a Gothic novel.

"I've instructed Murray to call for a hansom to take you home. It should arrive directly. If you have something important to say to me, I suggest you do so within"—he withdrew his pocket watch from his waistcoat and gave it a cursory glance—"the next five minutes."

Her frown deepened. "That was my intention." She certainly hadn't traveled all the way to Fleet Street to bombard her former beau with garden-variety chitter-chatter. "Although… I'm afraid it's rather complicated."

"Shall I simplify the matter? You're clearly here as a matter of duty. I might have predicted as much." His mouth curved into a humorless smile. "You're nothing if not a dutiful daughter."

"I hope I am, sir, but I don't see—"

"I gather your parents aren't pleased that our…association…has come to an end."

She didn't deny it.

"And they've instructed you to repair the breach, have they?" He moved as if to rise.

Sophie anticipated him, standing in a rustle of starched petticoats. She wasn't about to let any man loom over her and read her a lecture, least of all Mr. Edward Sharpe.

"Let me set your mind at ease, ma'am." He stood to his full and not inconsiderable height. "There's nothing between us to repair. There never was."

She swallowed back an acute spasm of disappointment. "In other words—"

"In other words, Miss Appersett, I was as amenable to putting an end to our courtship as you were." He came out from behind his desk, moving as if to escort her to the door.

"If you require me to explain such to your parents, I'd be delighted to do so. Now, if you would be so kind as to gather your things—"

"You're wrong. My parents didn't instruct me to make amends with you. Quite the opposite. They may not be happy with my decision to end our courtship, but they fully support it."

"Ah."

"It's the truth. Whatever their failings, my mother and father would never force me to marry a gentleman I didn't like."

Mr. Sharpe went still. He gave her a look that was hard to read. "You have me at a disadvantage, ma'am. I don't recall having asked you to marry me."

Sophie blushed to the roots of her hair. She opened her mouth to make a sharp retort, but the words, once summoned, wouldn't come. Something in his face stopped her. It was just a flicker. She might well have imagined it. Nevertheless…

She took a step toward him, brows knitting with concern. "I hurt you, didn't I?"

He failed to conceal a flinch before turning back to his desk. He straightened a stack of papers that didn't need straightening. "You assume a great deal."

"I didn't know I had the power to hurt you."

"You don't."

"Nothing else could have provoked you to say something so ungentlemanly."

"We're not in a drawing room in Mayfair, Miss Appersett." He paused before adding gruffly, "But if I've offended you, I beg your pardon. Now, if you'll gather your things. I see no reason to continue—"

"Please. Please, don't apologize. I could do with a little plain speaking between us. Indeed, it's the sole reason I've come here." She took another step in his direction. "You see, Mr. Sharpe…I have a proposition for you."

Ned's gaze jerked to hers. A *proposition*?

What the devil?

His breath stopped at the various implications of her words. None of them were good.

He wished it were otherwise. That she'd come here for—What? To tell him she was sorry she'd ended their courtship? That she'd made a mistake? Sentimental nonsense. He'd learned long ago that there was no point indulging such thinking. No purpose in sticking his head in the sand. It was better to face reality. Even if that reality was bleak and painful and deeply disappointing. Even if that reality wounded his pride.

So, Sophia Appersett was as mercenary in her own way as her parents were. As mercenary as she'd accused him of being himself.

Did she need money? Is that what this was? A ploy to gain some manner of compensation? He hadn't offered marriage to her, it was true, but that was no reason her father couldn't threaten a breach of promise suit.

The very idea made his blood pump hot with outrage. Good God, but he was no untried youth to be manipulated thus.

"A proposition," he repeated in a voice of dangerous calm.

"In a manner of speaking."

Ned's heart hardened into an unforgiving lump in his chest. "And the terms?"

Miss Appersett stared at him blankly. And then realization lit in her eyes. She gave a soft huff of annoyance. "Not a business proposition. A proposition about how we might deal better together. What I'm proposing is...honesty."

His already heated blood simmered to a boil. "If you're implying I've been anything less—"

"Perhaps *candor* would be a better word," she said hastily.

He glowered at her. "Go on."

"When we met in the park last Monday, I told you we had nothing at all in common. Do you remember?"

"I'm not likely to forget."

"Yes, well, my point is that, upon reflection, I realized I've no way of ascertaining the truth of that statement. Not when we've never even talked to each other."

"We've never talked to each other?" He made no effort to conceal his impatience. "And how, pray, have we been communicating these past two months if not by talking? Through smoke signals?"

"We haven't *talked*. Not in any meaningful way. Indeed, I scarcely know a thing about you. Least of all why a gentleman of your disposition should ever wish to court a girl like me."

A gentleman of his disposition.

Was that a carefully coded way of saying that he was crass? Vulgar? Unable to appreciate fine things? He stifled the urge to tell her that even a common working man could recognize quality when he saw it.

"There's no great mystery to it," he said. "You're a beautiful creature."

Miss Appersett's lips compressed into a thin line. She didn't look pleased by the compliment. Rather the opposite. She gathered her things from the chair by his desk. "My sister is the acknowledged beauty of the family. Far more beautiful than I."

Ned refrained from stating the obvious. There was no comparison. How could there be? Miss Emily was a chit of barely nineteen. A vacuous, overdelicate girl—rather like a hollow porcelain ornament one might place on a mantelshelf.

Miss Appersett had a delicacy to her countenance as well, but there was nothing anemic about her beauty. There was a depth to her. A certain sensible pragmatism which—on occasion—had given way to a merry laugh or a smile of genuine warmth. He'd never been on the receiving end of such smiles, but until their ill-fated meeting in Hyde Park, he'd had every reason to hope.

No, Sophia Appersett was no porcelain figure to be placed on a shelf. He'd recognized it from the first moment he saw her. If hardship came, she wouldn't shatter into a million useless pieces. To the lucky gentleman who won her, she'd be a friend. A partner.

"Your sister has many admirable qualities, I'm sure," he said.

"She's the belle of Derbyshire." Miss Appersett tugged on her worn leather gloves. "A beauty of some repute."

"Is she indeed."

"If that was your only requirement, you would have done better to court her."

He gave a derisive snort. "I doubt she'd have had me."

Miss Appersett's eyes flew to his, a hint of accusation in her gaze. And something else, too. Some flash of emotion he couldn't interpret.

His heart gave a queer double-thump. "Besides, beauty wasn't my only requirement."

"No? What other reason could you have had for approaching my father?"

He shrugged. "I suppose I thought I could make you happy. Apparently, I was wrong."

A shadow of vulnerability passed over Miss Appersett's face. For the barest moment, she looked far younger than the self-possessed lady he'd lately squired about town. "If I hadn't ended our courtship, would you have done?" she asked.

A damnably awkward question. Especially when he'd already agreed that they didn't suit. He ran his hand over the back of his neck. "Perhaps. Eventually. I don't know."

"You can't have been very comfortable."

"Is courtship meant to be comfortable in your world?"

Any response Miss Appersett might have given was arrested by a firm rap on the office door. It shook the doorframe and rattled the glass, causing them to jump away from each other as if they'd been caught in the midst of committing a crime.

Walter Murray popped his ginger head into the room. "Forgive the interruption. The carriage has arrived. Shall I have the driver wait?"

Ned silently cursed his friend's bad timing. "We'll be right down."

Walter withdrew, leaving the door open behind him. A not-so-subtle hint that Ned must observe the proprieties. As if he needed reminding. Miss Appersett's visit already verged on the scandalous. It was going to be a pretty trick to bundle her into the hansom and send her back to Green Street without arousing any more attention.

She seemed to read his mind. "It was unwise of me to come here."

"Yes. And, if I may add, very unlike you, Miss Appersett."

Her expression cooled. "And may *I* add, Mr. Sharpe, that you don't know me at all."

He inclined his head in silent acknowledgment. An excruciatingly civil gesture that was precariously close to mockery. "Indeed, ma'am." He held the door open for her, wide enough to accommodate her skirts.

But Miss Appersett made no move to exit. She merely stood there, her hands clutched in front of her and her bosom rising and falling on an agitated breath. Twin spots of color rose high in her cheeks. She looked rather magnificent. "In answer to your question," she said, "I don't know if courtship is comfortable in my world or anywhere. The truth is, you're the first gentleman who's ever asked leave to court me."

Ned's hand fell from the door. He couldn't have been more surprised if she'd hauled off and slapped him across the face.

Was it possible? Could it be true?

He cast his mind back to his first meeting with Sir William. Ned had called on him in Green Street. Had asked leave to court his eldest daughter. All the while, painfully aware that he was not quite one of them. Not quite good enough.

"*My daughters have many admirers, Mr. Sharpe,*" Sir William had said.

And yet...

He'd never explicitly stated that there were rivals for Miss Appersett's hand. He'd implied it, of course. Had made Ned feel he must compete. Must prove himself better than all the rest. Indeed, it was after that first meeting with Sir William that Ned had purchased that damned etiquette manual.

"No one?" Ned asked her. "In your entire three-and-twenty years? I find that hard to believe."

"Believe what you will," she said. And then: "I have no dowry, sir."

"I'm aware," he said. She made no reply. A long silence hung between them, prompting him to say, somewhat indecorously, "I understand that your father lost it on speculation."

Miss Appersett flinched. "Is that what he told you?"

"It isn't true?"

"Not precisely." She hesitated. "If you must know, my father used my dowry to have Appersett House fitted for gas."

Ned blinked. "He *what?*"

Her blush deepened. "It was once a showplace. One of the finest estates in Derbyshire. My father means to make it so again."

"At the cost of his daughters' dowries?"

"No," Miss Appersett said. "Just mine."

FOUR

Sophie allowed Mr. Sharpe to escort her from his office and back down the stairs. He said nothing to her. Not a grunt of acknowledgment when she thanked him for holding the door. Not a murmur of warning when she encountered an uneven step (though his hand did tighten on her elbow to guide her over it). Indeed, shortly after her disclosure about her dowry, he'd withdrawn behind his familiar wall of implacable silence.

Perhaps she'd confided too much? Or perhaps he was merely irritated that she'd kept him from his dinner engagement. Her visit had absorbed far more of his time than the five minutes he'd marked with his pocket watch.

By the time they emerged from the building, the sky had darkened and the fog had rolled in off the river. The glow of the gas lamps illuminated the street. A carriage awaited her there. But it was not a hansom cab or a brougham. It was a glossy black four-wheeler hitched to a team of matched bays.

She turned to Mr. Sharpe, a question in her eyes.

"It's my carriage," he said in an odd, flat voice. "Murray must have summoned it."

"Why ever would he do that?"

"Because he's meddling in things that don't concern him." Mr. Sharpe's face settled into an expression of grim resolve. He stepped forward, his hand still at her elbow. "Come. We shouldn't linger."

The footman on the box moved to descend, but Mr. Sharpe motioned for him to remain where he was. He opened the carriage door himself and set down the steps.

The coachman called out to him. "To Cheapside, Mr. Sharpe? By way of Green Street?"

Sophie stole a curious glance at Mr. Sharpe's face. *Cheapside?* Was that the location of his dinner party?

"Straight to Green Street, John." Mr. Sharpe assisted her into the carriage. "You can come back for me afterward."

"It's nearly quarter past, sir."

Mr. Sharpe grimaced. "Is it?" He checked his pocket watch. "Blast."

Sophie's cheeks warmed at his language.

He caught her gaze in the interior of the carriage. It was dimly lit by two softly flickering carriage lamps. "Miss Appersett, I'm at risk of being unforgivably late to an engagement. If you wouldn't mind—"

"Of course not," she said. "You're already late enough on my account."

He nodded once and, after a final word to the coachman, vaulted into the carriage and shut the door behind him.

Sophie moved her skirts out of the way as he took a seat across from her. The carriage rumbled forward, to Green Street presumably.

"Your parents will be expecting you?" he asked.

She shook her head. Mama and Papa didn't expect her home until nearer to midnight. "They believe I'm visiting Lady Dawlish."

"I see. And is Lady Dawlish aware of your deception?"

"I shouldn't think so. Her brother is lately returned from India. There's a reception for him tonight. A very large reception. My absence will hardly be remarked."

"You didn't wish to attend?"

"Not particularly." Sophie smoothed her skirts. "What about you?"

"What about me?"

"Your dinner engagement. Is it a formal party? Is that why you're so concerned with being late?"

He fell silent for several seconds. "It's a dinner party at my parent's house," he said at last.

She looked at him, bewildered. "In Cheapside?"

He gave a terse nod.

"But I thought your parents had retired to the country? Kent or Essex or somewhere."

"They have a house in Kent, it's true. They mean to retire there someday. Until then..." He shrugged.

Her sense of confusion only deepened. Mr. Sharpe had never mentioned his parents. Not directly, at any rate. She knew they were in trade. It was how they'd made their fortune. But those days were long past, surely? Papa had said something to that effect. Something about how he and Mama would never have to suffer the indignity of dealing with Mr. Sharpe's uncouth relations. "I'm sorry, but are you saying that your parents are presently living here? In London?"

"They have apartments above their draper's shop."

"And you never thought to mention that fact?"

He leaned back in his seat, stretching his legs out before him. "To you? Why should I have?"

"Because you were courting me. Presumably, if things had progressed, I would have been obliged to meet your parents."

"Would you have wanted to?"

"Naturally. And it needn't have waited. I would have been happy to meet them from the very first."

"Is that so?"

"Did I ever give you reason to doubt it?"

Another long pause. And then: "Perhaps you're right, Miss Appersett. Perhaps I don't know you at all."

"No, indeed," she said with some asperity. "You appear to be laboring under a misapprehension about my character."

"Which is?"

"That I'm a shallow, self-centered creature, too full of my own importance to see past the end of my nose."

"I assure you, ma'am, such thoughts never crossed my mind."

"Then why did you never talk to me?" She searched his face, what little she could see of it in the weak candlelight cast from the carriage lamps. "You're not ashamed of your origins, are you?"

He snorted. "Hardly. Just because I don't see fit to bandy my lack of pedigree about in the streets—"

"Confiding in me is a far way from the streets, Mr. Sharpe."

"Is that what you want from me, Miss Appersett? My confidences?"

"I'd like us to be candid with each other. To make an effort to understand one another." Her self-assuredness faltered. "Unless you truly don't wish to renew your addresses to me. In which case—"

"Candor," he repeated. "Very well." He folded his arms, his face growing solemn, as if he were contemplating his words with a greater than usual degree of care. "You asked me earlier why it was that I wished to court you. The answer I gave you was incomplete."

"You said it was because you thought me a beautiful creature."

"I did. But there are many beautiful ladies in London. I've never wished to court any of them before. With you, however, there was something different."

Sophie waited for him to explain, expecting she knew not what. Was it her intelligence that had appealed to him? Her grace and charm?

"I believe it was your dress that first caught my eye," he said.

She blinked. "I beg your pardon?"

"The gown you were wearing. A printed muslin, if I remember."

She knew the dress of which he spoke only too well. Her voice turned a trifle defensive. "What about it?"

"It was worn and faded and, like your chip bonnet, very obviously made over to look like new."

A mortified blush rose hot in her cheeks. "And that's why you asked leave to court me? Because I looked an absolute shag-rag?"

"You misunderstand me. You didn't look shabby at all. You were neat as a pin. And you stood there, on the promenade, so poised—so very regal—that you might have been one of the royal party."

Sophie didn't know what to say. Surely he must be teasing her? The royal party indeed. "Nonsense," she scoffed. "Mrs. Carstairs was dressed far better than I."

"And you shone her down."

Her face burned. Was he trying to put her out of countenance? "I doubt you even remember what I was wearing. How could you? It was months ago, long before we were courting."

"I'm the son of a draper, Miss Appersett. And a part owner of three cotton mills. Do you think I wouldn't recognized faded fabric?"

She bent her head, feeling more disappointed than she'd imagined possible. "That's the truth of it, then? Why you asked leave to pay your addresses? Because I was so obviously in reduced circumstances?"

He gave a low growl of frustration. "No. No, that wasn't it at all."

"Then why?"

"Because it didn't matter to you. You weren't cringing with shame. You weren't putting on airs. You were simply...you. A lady through and through. And one I very much wished to know better."

Ned waited for her to say something. Anything. But Miss Appersett merely looked at him. She appeared to be nonplussed. As if his words had taken her completely by surprise. "That's the truth of it, at any rate," he grumbled. "Make of it what you will."

The carriage clattered along the cobbled street. They must be fairly close to Miss Appersett's house in Mayfair by now.

It wouldn't be much longer. He could deposit her in Green Street and correct course to Cheapside. His parents were probably waiting dinner for him. It wasn't like him to be late. And certainly not by more than a quarter of an hour.

Damn Walter and his interfering!

What the devil had he thought would happen when he summoned Ned's personal carriage instead of a hansom? Did he think Ned would feel compelled to renew his addresses to Miss Appersett? That he would invite her to meet his parents? That he would propose?

No doubt Walter saw her arrival at their offices as a positive occurrence. Ned wasn't convinced. When she'd broken things off with him, she'd been so sure of herself. So thoroughly decided against him.

What had prompted her to come to Fleet Street?

Granted, they didn't know each other very well—unless one counted the many civilities they'd exchanged during their courtship—but it seemed that such a risk was entirely out of character for Miss Appersett. She'd always been so ladylike. So very proper.

"Do you have anything you wish to say to me?" he asked. "Now that we're speaking candidly with one another?"

She turned her head to look out the window. There was precious little to see in all the fog, save the intermittent glow of the gas lamps. "What would you like to know?"

"Why the change of heart?"

"I've had a week to think it over. I realized I was too impulsive."

"That morning in Hyde Park? It seemed to me that you were being honest."

She turned her face from the window. "I *was* being honest. Just not very wise."

"So…not really a change of heart, then."

"More like a change of mind."

Ned appreciated her honesty, but her words stung all the same. She had no dowry, and therefore no practical choice. Which begged the question: what sort of sapskull would use his eldest daughter's marriage portion to have gaslight installed?

It was not that modernizations were uncommon. Far from it. In London, many townhouses featured gas wall sconces and gasoliers. But to have a country estate fitted for gas—especially when that estate was the size and antiquity of Appersett House—seemed absolute folly. Not only was there the expense of the installation, there was also the small matter of where the gas would originate. In London, it was provided by a central gas works. But in rural Derbyshire? Sir William would have had to commission a private gas plant.

Was it any wonder he needed his daughters to marry into money?

"What prompted this change of mind?" Ned asked. "Was it your parents?"

"No. Though they weren't best pleased with me. My father bellowed until he was red in the face. And my mother, she—" Miss Appersett broke off. Her brow furrowed, her gloved hands clasped tight in her lap. "You must understand, Mr. Sharpe. Girls in my situation hardly ever marry for love. We haven't that luxury. We marry for comfort and security."

"And to benefit your family."

She didn't deny it. There was no reason to do so. They both knew why her father had permitted him to court her. "If we're lucky, we come to respect our husbands. To like them, even."

"But you don't like me. As we've established."

"I don't *know* you. Which is why I came today, ill-advised as my visit was. I thought, if we could just talk. If we could just dispense with all of the stifling formality. I thought there was a chance that I'd been mistaken. About us being ill-suited, I mean. After all, I had no way of knowing—" She broke off. "Good heavens. How I'm rambling on." She turned back to the carriage window. "I promised myself, if we ever met again, I wouldn't talk so much."

"Did you?" He could see her face reflected in the glass, pale and solemn. "I always enjoyed the sound of your voice."

"You certainly heard enough of it."

The carriage rolled to a halt with a jolt and a clatter of hooves. Ned glanced out the window. It was difficult to make anything out in the fog, but it appeared that John Coachman had taken them to the mews. A discreet and sensible fellow. Ned wouldn't have credited it.

"Is this all right?" he asked.

She nodded. "There's a gate at the end of the garden."

The carriage rocked as the footman clambered down from the box. A second later, he was at the door. Ned heard him clear his throat.

"Well, I suppose this is goodbye," Miss Appersett said. "Unless..."

Unless. There was a wealth of meaning in the word. It was chance and opportunity, risk and possible reward. It was also an olive branch of a sort. All he need do was reach out and take it. Ned swallowed his pride. "What would you like me to do, Miss Appersett?"

Some of the tension went out of her face. He hadn't realized it was there until it was gone.

Good Lord, had she really believed he'd deny her? If so, she'd vastly underrated her charms. Either that or vastly overrated his strength of will.

She lowered her voice. "Firstly, I would like you to call me Sophie."

Sophie. His heart thumped hard. "And secondly?"

"I would like you to come to Appersett House for Christmas, as we originally planned."

The footman rapped lightly on the outside of the carriage door. "Sir?"

They must be in danger of drawing attention. A legitimate concern, but for the moment Ned didn't care. He held Sophie Appersett's gaze. "Very well," he said brusquely. "Is there a thirdly?"

Her dark brows knit. The tension and worry were back. The visible uncertainty about her future and about the future of her family. But there was something more there now. A glimmer of hope in her chocolate brown eyes that gave him hope in return. "That all depends," she said, "on what happens in Derbyshire."

FIVE

Derbyshire, England
December, 1861

Sophie gazed out the rain-streaked window of the railway car. The passing scenery was bleak and wet and oh so familiar. She knew this part of the Derbyshire countryside like the back of her hand.

In a half hour, they would arrive at the modest station in the village of Milton St. Edmunds. From there, the family carriage would convey them to the lush—and quite isolated—valley where Appersett House had resided in stately splendor since the turn of the sixteenth century. Papa had sent a wire from Waterloo Station. All should be in readiness for them.

She shifted in her seat, striving for a more comfortable position. Emily's head was heavy on her shoulder. Sophie dared not wake her. Her sister had only just been lulled to sleep by the motion of the train, drifting off against Sophie's side mid-complaint. Sophie had no doubt that, if awakened, she'd resume her litany of misery without missing a beat.

The Christmas party was ruined, or so Emily had been insisting since they departed London.

For once, she wasn't exaggerating.

Prince Albert was dead. He'd passed away late Saturday evening, reportedly from typhoid fever. The bells of St. Paul's had rung out at midnight, announcing the mournful event to the world.

Only two days later, the newspapers were filled with recollections of him. Sophie still couldn't quite believe it.

Her family wasn't so exalted as to have known him personally. Indeed, she'd only ever seen him once. It was at the opening of the Horticultural Gardens at South Kensington. The day she'd first met Mr. Sharpe. Prince Albert had been presiding over the event. She'd thought him a noble figure. A man of bearing who, along with the Queen, represented the very best of English dignity and good sense.

Upon hearing the news, the residents of Green Street had been thrown into an uproar.

"*No one will come to Appersett House for Christmas now,*" Emily had wailed. "*The holiday is ruined!*"

Papa's reaction to the tragic news had been no better. He'd bemoaned the expense of the Christmas festivities, all come to nothing now that the nation was plunged into mourning.

"*I won't wear black,*" Emily had said, stamping her slippered foot. "*I simply won't do it!*"

As usual, it was Mama who calmed the troubled waters. "*We shan't be obliged to. But I do think a black armband would not be amiss.*"

Papa had nodded vigorously. "*Quite right, my dear. We must show the proper respect.*"

Sophie's own black armband was presently sliding down to her elbow, courtesy of Emily's head. She wondered if the servants had already donned armbands of their own? It was very likely. Their housekeeper was a stickler when it came to such things. No doubt she'd run up the armbands herself on the sewing machine they'd purchased last year. Yet another modern invention which Papa had deemed a necessity.

She glanced at her mother. Unlike Sophie and her sister, Mama was garbed in unrelieved black. She was seated across from them in the railway carriage, her needlework on her lap. Papa had departed some time ago for the smoking car. It was all to the good. He was as restless as Emily on long journeys and, inevitably, would turn his attention to arguing with Sophie about some triviality or other.

At least, he could no longer reproach her over Mr. Sharpe.

"Sophie, my love," Mama said as she tied off a thread. "Wake your sister, won't you?"

Sophie gave Emily a little jostle.

"Are we there yet?" Emily asked as she sat up.

"Nearly," Sophie said. "Here. Let me re-pin your plaits." Emily obediently bent her head while Sophie made swift work of smoothing and pinning her elaborately braided coiffure.

Sophie's own hair needed no attention. She'd rolled it into a large chignon at the nape of her neck earlier that morning and secured it with over a dozen pins. It wasn't likely to budge in a high wind, let alone during a railway journey.

In short order the train arrived at the station. Papa joined them to disembark, smelling strongly of tobacco and spirits. It was raining dreadfully. An icy wind whistled down the platform, whipping at Sophie's heavy skirts and biting at her face. Papa shouted to the porters about their luggage and then, with a great deal of fanfare, they all bundled into the carriage and began the last leg of the journey home.

The roads were awash in mud, and none more so than the rural track that led through the valley. Appersett House rose up amongst the wooded landscape, an enormous structure of graceful lines wrought in honey-colored stone.

It hadn't always looked so elegant. During the seventeenth century, the ruin of the original house had been torn down and the whole of it rebuilt in the fashionable Palladian style. All stately windows and engaged columns, set back from a pristine vista of rolling green lawn.

Even our ancestors didn't know when to stop improving.

The carriage rolled up the long drive, coming to a stop in front of the wide, sweeping front steps. The ground was the consistency of pea soup.

"It needs to be re-graveled," Papa grumbled as he handed them down from the carriage.

Sophie pretended she didn't hear him. The last thing she wanted to think about at the moment was the family's finances—or lack thereof. What she needed was a warm fire and a hot cup of tea. She followed her mother and sister into the house where both awaited her, along with hot buttered scones and freshly baked lemon cakes.

For all its splendor—and for all Papa's endless modernizations—Appersett House was, quite simply, home. The gaslight cast a soft glow on richly carpeted rooms filled with overstuffed chairs, plump sofas, and tufted footstools edged in silken fringe. Every imaginable surface was covered in meaningful bric-a-brac. There were crystal animal figurines, blue and white porcelain, and silver epergnes and branches of candles. Gilt-trimmed clocks chimed from the mantelshelves and paintings of illustrious ancestors graced the silk-papered walls.

Granted, the carpet and furnishings had seen better days, but the faded grandeur of Appersett House was what Sophie loved best about it. The rooms were cozy rather than austere, perfect for snuggling up with a favorite book or dozing off beside a crackling fire.

"There's so much decorating to do before the guests arrive," Mama said as they finished their tea.

Emily licked lemon icing from her fingers. "If we have any guests."

"No one has sent their regrets, have they?" Sophie asked.

Mama returned her painted porcelain teacup to the tea tray. "Not as yet, but it's a fortnight before they're scheduled to arrive. We may yet hear from them."

And hear from them they did

Nearly half of their guests felt the death of Prince Albert significant enough to disrupt their holiday plans. Letters began arriving within the week, sending excuses and regrets and, in one case, a mild reproof that their Christmas revels hadn't been cancelled altogether.

It was a catastrophe, at least as far as her father and sister were concerned. Even her mother lamented the great waste of so much food and the expense of all the various trifles purchased to make the holiday memorable for their guests.

Over the course of the next week, Sophie thought on the matter at length. She was not impulsive by nature. She'd spent all her life doing exactly what she was told. But society was evolving at an accelerated rate. This was the modern age, after all. And surely the gentry were no different from any other organic beings. They must adapt to changing circumstances or risk extinction in one form or other.

Besides, weren't she and Mr. Sharpe supposed to be open and honest with each other? To dispense with the stiff formality that had characterized the beginning of their courtship and get to know each other for who they really were?

What better way to do so than to invite his parents to join their Christmas party?

And if they were to come, surely there could be no objection to inviting others of their class.

The prospect sent a nervous hum through Sophie's veins. There was much that could go wrong. But it was Christmas and, despite her concerns, she felt rather optimistic.

Having made her decision, she wrapped an old cashmere shawl loosely round her shoulders and hurried down the stairs to find her mother.

She was seated at the little carved walnut secretary in the morning room, engaged in writing a letter.

"Mama?" Sophie ducked inside, shutting the white-paneled door firmly behind her.

The morning room was Mama's private domain. It was a thoroughly feminine space, with walls papered in pale blue watered silk and floors carpeted in patterned floral Aubusson. Bright sunlight filtered in through a bank of windows.

"Hmm?" Mama kept writing.

Sophie came to stand beside her. "Will you allow me to try and make up the numbers?"

Her mother's pen flew across the page. "If you like."

"I have an idea. Papa and Emily won't care for it, but it makes perfect sense—"

"Sophie, love, I'm trying to finish this letter to your uncle. It absolutely must go out in the morning post."

"Then I have your approval?"

"Always," she said, adding, "Do shut the door when you leave."

As permission went, Sophie doubted whether it would stand up to scrutiny. However, given their circumstances, it was enough. She pressed a swift kiss to her mother's rose-perfumed cheek and then, in a swish of petticoats, bounded back upstairs to write a few letters of her own.

The poorly sprung four-wheeler they'd hired at the railway station in Milton St. Edmunds gave another bone-rattling jolt as it trundled through the mud. The rain had stopped for the moment, but the rural track, which the coachman had assured them led to Appersett House, was made no more hospitable by it. The terrain was uneven, the ground riddled with potholes.

"It was very civil of her to extend the invitation," Ned's mother said for what must be the hundredth time. "But I can't feel easy about any of this."

Ned's father nodded. "She's a baronet's daughter," he added, also for the hundredth time. As if it explained everything.

Ned looked across the interior of the carriage at his parents. They were a severe, dignified couple, both of them handsomely dressed and both of them long past their middle years.

They'd had him late in life, the only one of their children to live past the age of three.

From boyhood, they had reposed all their hopes in him. And, as he'd grown, they'd seen in him the manifestation of a lifetime of sacrifice and hard work. They would sooner sever ties with him forever than harm his ascent into polite society.

Perhaps this wasn't a good idea after all. His parents would be uncomfortable. Hell, he was going to be uncomfortable himself. It was unavoidable when people of their sort mingled with the upper classes. "It's too late to turn back now. Mr.

Murray will have already arrived. If we don't appear, he's likely to send out a search party for us."

His mother gave a low cluck of disapproval. "I still can't credit his being invited. Doesn't your young lady know what a scapegrace he is?"

"She's not his young lady," his father said. "If she were, we'd have met her afore now."

Ned felt a faint flicker of guilt. He hadn't introduced Sophie to his parents yet, it was true. He'd been waiting until things were formalized between them. Until she consented to be his wife. In the meanwhile, there'd been no point in getting his parents' hopes up, nor in subjecting them to the poisonous barbs of the beau monde. He'd been determined to navigate these deep waters alone. To sink or swim on his own.

A wise decision, as it turned out, given that she'd broken things off with him.

And now, there was every chance she'd do so again.

He'd be a fool to ignore the facts. The fate of their relationship hinged on this Christmas house party. Or, more precisely, on whether or not, in the next ten days, he could make Sophie Appersett like him a little. A grim reality, but there it was.

When her letter arrived, inviting both his parents and Walter Murray to Derbyshire, he'd been inclined to write back immediately and tell her it wouldn't do. His parents weren't poor, not by any means, but they were of humble origins. And they were in trade. He knew firsthand how the gentry behaved toward such people. He had no wish to expose his mother and father to their derision.

His parents were of the same mind, albeit for different reasons. They were adamant that their presence would harm his chances. It would be much better, his father had said, if Sir William and his lady wife never met them at all. Much better if Ned were evaluated on his own merits than if he were viewed as no better than a Cheapside draper's son.

It troubled Ned how readily they assumed they'd have no place in his life once he married. As if he would sacrifice his own mother and father on the altar of social acceptance. He never would. And he damn well wouldn't permit them to sacrifice themselves.

"Not his young lady?" his mother echoed in disbelief.

"No, mother, she's not," Ned said firmly. "Not now. Possibly not ever."

His mother snorted. "She'd be a fool to refuse you." There was a thread of scorn in her voice, as if Sophie had already rejected him out of hand. "Haven't all the girls in Cheapside been chasing after you these many years and more? Girls from good families—prosperous families—with a sight more to their name than aristocratic airs and graces. You could have your pick of them."

Ned removed his hat, running a restless hand over his hair. "It's a Christmas party. That's all. Let's not make more if it than it is."

"A Christmas party at the country home of a baronet," his father remarked to his mother. "Hard to make more of that."

"And Walter Murray's to be there as well? I trust he's not angling after the younger sister."

Good God. Ned certainly hoped not. "He's helping make up the numbers. I understand the village vicar will be there as well, along with his wife and sister. It won't all be the gentry. And even if it were, you're every bit as respectable as—"

"Oh, my heavens," his mother breathed. "Is *that* Appersett House?"

Ned was in the backward-facing seat and had to twist round to see properly. His mouth went dry at the sight of the coldly elegant Palladian mansion looming up before them. He'd expected something spectacular. Appersett House had a much-vaunted reputation for its beauty. But he wasn't prepared for the awe-inspiring dignity of all that curving honey-colored stone.

"I assume it is," he said. "Unless we've taken a wrong a turn somewhere."

Ned's father had gone a little pale. So had his mother. She scanned the gravel drive. "Which one is she, Ned?"

Ned looked out the window as the carriage came to a halt. "I don't see Miss Appersett, or her parents."

Not that much was visible amongst the flurry of liveried servants unloading trunks and stablemen unhitching horses. The guests he did see were all bundled up in dark wool topcoats and voluminous cloaks, their heads covered in tall beaver hats and fussy feather-trimmed bonnets. He supposed he and his parents looked little different as they climbed out of their hired coach.

A footman appeared at the door to assist them down. "Welcome to Appersett House."

It was a sentiment echoed by the elderly butler who ushered them into the marble entry hall. Sir William and Lady Appersett were poised to receive their guests there, along with Miss Appersett's sister, Emily. But it was Sophie herself who crossed the hall to greet them, looking warm and radiant in a dress of russet-colored velvet, her dark hair swept up in a glass-beaded net. She sparkled in the light cast from a magnificent crystal gasolier suspended low from the ceiling.

Ned's pulse quickened. How well she looked. How perfectly at ease amidst so much splendor. "Miss Appersett."

"Mr. Sharpe." She turned to his parents and smiled. "And you must be Mr. and Mrs. Sharpe?"

Ned quickly dispensed with the introductions. His parents had assumed their all-too-familiar mantle of cool civility. They were not the warmest people at the best of times. Not even with him. But when they felt themselves at any sort of disadvantage, their temperature always dropped by several more degrees.

"I'm so pleased you could come," Sophie said. "I trust you had a pleasant journey?"

"Very pleasant," his father replied stiffly.

"And very wet," Ned added. "Though the rain seems to have stopped for now."

"Oh, yes," Sophie said. "There's a distinct chill in the air. And did you see the clouds? It means the snow will start soon. Tomorrow, probably, or the day after."

Ned's mother was looking at Sophie as keenly as she often looked at a bolt of fabric when assessing it for flaws. "You have a fine home, Miss Appersett."

Sophie's smile faded a little under his mother's scrutiny. "Thank you, ma'am. It's my father's pride and joy. Once you've rested, I'm sure he'll want to show you all the latest modernizations. Won't you, Papa?"

Sir William approached to greet them, seemingly at the urging of his lady wife. Like Sophie and her mother, he wore a black armband, a symbol of mourning at the passing of the Prince Consort. On Sir William, however, the scrap of fabric appeared almost ostentatious. He was a proud man. Rather too proud, Ned thought, given the circumstances.

"Mr. and Mrs. Sharpe," he said. "You are very welcome."

As his parents talked with Sir William and Lady Appersett, Ned found himself standing beside Sophie, a little distance away. He looked down at her, uncertain what to say.

She appeared to be equally uncertain. "It wasn't too great an inconvenience, was it?" she asked at last. "Bringing your parents, I mean."

"Not at all. They were pleased to accept your invitation. Though it may well prove to be an awkward visit if our courtship comes to nothing." He instantly regretted his words. What was he thinking to be so dry, so flippant, about something so important?

Sophie didn't seem to mind. "I'm resolved not to think of what will happen after Christmas. Even if the whole world were to disappear in a puff of smoke—and this house along with it."

"That bad, is it?"

"You can't really expect me to answer that, sir."

"Can't I? And here I thought we were supposed to be candid with each other."

"Not in the hall," she said. "Not as the guests are arriving."

"When?"

She looked away from him to smile briefly at an elderly lady and gentleman who had just been admitted by the butler "Are you an early riser?"

"Always."

"We can go for a walk in the morning, if you like. I'm up at sunrise. There's no one about then."

He had no opportunity to answer. Sir William and Lady Appersett moved off to greet the new arrivals and his parents drifted back, looking only slightly less uncomfortable.

Sophie gave them a bright smile—far brighter than she'd ever given him. "We have mulled wine and cake in the drawing room," she told them. "But you must be tired from your journey. And I daresay you'll wish to freshen up. I can have tea sent to your rooms if you'd prefer?"

His mother drew herself up with offended dignity. "We shall join the other guests, Miss Appersett."

"Of course. Mr. Murray is already there, I believe. He'll be glad to know you've arrived safely." She summoned a footman. "Will you show Mr. and Mrs. Sharpe to the drawing room?"

"Aren't you coming?" Ned asked.

"Not yet. I must remain with my parents until the last of the guests arrive. But please, do go ahead, Mr. Sharpe."

He bent his head, his voice sinking to an undertone. "You'd better call me Edward. Or Ned, if you like. It will be confusing, otherwise. Too many Mr. Sharpes."

Sophie looked up at him. Her cheeks flushed pink. "Very well," she said. "Ned."

SIX

Sophie rose at dawn to wash and dress. Mr. Sharpe—or Ned, as he'd asked her to call him—hadn't precisely said he'd meet her for a walk, but she was taking no chances.

The house party was already in chaos. Papa was in a foul mood about some of the guests she'd invited. And Mama was at sixes and sevens trying to placate him at the same time she managed everything else. As for Emily…

Well. She'd taken a liking to Mr. Murray of all people.

Sophie was dumbfounded. If she'd known there was a chance her sister would strike up a flirtation with the man, she'd never have invited him. Her parents were banking on Emily marrying a title, for heaven's sake. If she squandered her chances with a stonemason's son, Sophie would never hear the end of it.

She fastened up the bodice of her heavy woolen dress and slipped her arms through the wide sleeves of her paletot. With any luck, no one would be up but the servants.

The gaslight in the wall sconces that lined the corridor outside her room was turned on low. It was just enough light to find her way to the stairs. She held her skirts as she descended two flights to the entry hall.

And then she stopped short.

"Good morning!" Emily said brightly. She was bundled up in a fur-trimmed cloak, her hair disposed in sable ringlets beneath a matching fur and velvet hat.

So much for privacy, Sophie thought grimly. She crossed the hall, frowning. "What on earth are you doing up at this hour?"

"Meeting someone."

"Who?"

"Mr. Murray." Emily stifled a giggle. "Of the firm of Sharpe, Murray, and Cratchit."

Sophie gave a quick glance around before turning on her sister. "Emmy, hush! This is no laughing matter." She caught her arm and marched her away from the stairs. "Are you telling me that you've made an assignation with Mr. Murray?"

Emily tugged her arm free from Sophie's grasp. "How dastardly you make it sound! We're only going out to collect some Christmas greenery."

"Christmas greenery my great aunt Sally. Emmy, have you no care for your reputation?"

"Why? Is Mr. Murray a rake? Will he ravish me at the first opportunity? Really, Sophie. The man's a guest here, he's hardly likely to—"

"He doesn't have to *do* anything. The mere hint of impropriety would be enough to—"

"Pish-tosh. It's all perfectly innocent. A mere holiday flirtation."

Sophie made an effort to gentle her voice. "Flirtation is not a game, dear. Not when you're an eligible young lady and he's an eligible man. You mustn't raise his expectations."

Emily gave a scornful laugh. "As if I would lower myself! He's a tradesman, Sophie. A rough fellow of absolutely no account except for money. Besides, just because Papa said you must marry beneath you, it doesn't follow that I must. My prospects aren't so grim as yours."

Sophie saw no humor in her sister's words. She didn't suppose she was meant to. "I'd no idea you had such fixed opinions on the subject."

"Someone in the family must uphold the old standards. With you haring off to Fleet Street of an evening, I daresay it must be me."

"Lord help us all."

Emily's delicate features transformed into a scowl. "What are you doing up anyway? Not going down to the kitchens, I hope. Mama has already sorted the menus. And we none of us want any of your little economies this Christmas. We're meant to be enjoying ourselves."

A gentleman cleared his throat. "Forgive the interruption, ladies."

Sophie froze, and Emily along with her. They turned in unison to find Mr. Murray standing near the servant's door that led down to the kitchens. He was dressed in a heavy wool topcoat and trousers. His head was uncovered, his carroty hair slightly disheveled.

Sophie wondered how long he'd been there.

"Mr. Murray," Emily said in tones of exaggerated relief. "There you are. I've been waiting an age."

Mr. Murray's mouth curved into a wry smile that didn't quite meet his eyes. "Have you? How unfortunate."

Sophie regarded him with reluctant sympathy. He'd heard everything, of course. Every hurtful, judgmental word. "We'll be going out to gather greenery with the rest of the guests tomorrow, sir. You'll wish to join us then, I presume."

Mr. Murray inclined his head. "I would at that, Miss Appersett. No point in going out twice."

Emily opened her mouth to object. "But—"

"And you'll be returning to your room, won't you, dear?" Sophie held Emily's gaze. "It's too early to be tramping about out of doors. I'm sure you agree."

Emily's eyes narrowed. She glared at Mr. Murray a moment before turning the full force of her fury on her sister. "Very well. No one's up at this hour but servants and common people anyway. I should have known—"

"Emmy," Sophie said, a warning note in her voice. "Not another word."

Emily clamped her mouth shut. She cast another dark glance at Mr. Murray before spinning round in a swirl of fur-trimmed velvet and flouncing up the stairs.

When she was well out of sight, Sophie turned to Mr. Murray. She wouldn't apologize for her sister. Not to anyone, least of all a man who was practically a stranger to her. Still...

"She's very young," she said.

Mr. Murray's lips quirked. "And very decided in her opinions."

"It was wrong of you to arrange to meet with her. I can't imagine what you were thinking."

"Do you know," he said, "at the moment, I can't remember myself."

"You mustn't do so again. If anyone were to find out, the consequences wouldn't be to your liking."

"In other words, I'd end up married to the little viper, and she to me."

Sophie's lips compressed. "She's not a viper, Mr. Murray. She's a willful child, that's all."

"She's nineteen. Scarcely a child. But I won't argue with you. There seems little point in doing so. Your sister has the measure of me—and of Sharpe, too. I only wonder that you don't feel the same. Or is it that you hide it better?"

Sophie stiffened. "My feelings about Mr. Sharpe are none of your concern."

Mr. Murray smiled again. "Fair enough." He moved away from the door. "He's in the kitchen, in case you're interested. Mrs. Phillips was kind enough to feed us. Sharpe stayed behind for a second helping—or so he said. I expect he's waiting for you."

Sophie's heart fluttered on an unexpected rush of pleasure. He'd remembered about their walk after all.

She inclined her head. Mr. Murray bowed in return before taking his leave. His face was set in stone as he ascended the stairs. She supposed he was embarrassed about what Emily had said about him. Embarrassed and angry. Hopefully such feelings would prompt him to steer clear of her sister for the remainder of his visit.

The party was going to be difficult enough as it was. The guests were already morose over the death of Prince Albert. It hadn't helped that the local vicar, Mr. Hubbard, had droned on about it last evening after dinner. By the time he'd finished his sermon, no one was much in the mood for merrymaking.

And Mr. and Mrs. Sharpe certainly didn't appear to like her overmuch. Quite the reverse. Sophie had the distinct feeling that she'd been weighed, measured, and found wanting. Indeed, nothing she'd done all evening had seemed to be right in their eyes. Every word exchanged with Ned—and there hadn't been many—had earned her a glacial glance from his mother.

Was this why young ladies were told never to marry outside of their class? Was it simply an unworkable proposition?

She'd been puzzling over it most of the night. Tossing and turning in bed, reminding herself of how awkward her first two months of courtship with Ned had been. They hadn't talked. They hadn't laughed. They'd merely gone through the motions. Walks in the park, visits to Cremorne Gardens, or to hear a recital. He'd been her escort, nothing more. Not once had she felt a deeper sense of connection.

Was she a fool to think she'd find it now he was here in Derbyshire? What if the pair of them simply had no affinity for each other?

It was a very real possibility, but she couldn't entertain it. She was determined to do her duty to her family. She wouldn't make a martyr of herself. Nowhere near it. But if something could be salvaged between her and Edward Sharpe—even if it were just friendship—she would accept him as her suitor. As her husband.

It would have to be enough.

She proceeded through the servant's door off the main hall, descending a narrow flight of stairs down to the kitchens. They were spacious and bright, filled with the fragrance of freshly baked bread, hot coffee, and eggs and bacon. Maids and footmen bustled about, mumbling "good morning, miss" to Sophie as they passed.

Ned was standing near the ovens, exchanging easy words with the cook, Mrs. Phillips, as she stirred a pot of porridge. When he caught sight of Sophie, his expression became at once less open. More serious.

"Miss Appersett," he said. "Good morning."

"Mr. Sharpe." She bent her head in greeting as she walked past him, moving away from the prying eyes of Mrs. Phillips and the rest of the kitchen staff. A door off the kitchens led to the yard. She opened it and ducked outside, relieved to discover that Ned had followed in her wake.

He shut the door behind him. "I didn't know if you'd come."

"Nor I you," she said. "Let's away from the house, shall we? The servants have enough to gossip about this morning."

He fell into step beside her. "I gather you're referring to Murray's ill-conceived meeting with your sister."

"You knew about that?"

"He told me this morning. I advised him to leave her alone, for whatever that's worth."

"I'm sure he meant no harm." Sophie wondered who she was trying to convince. "It's not likely to come to anything, in any case. I expect they'll avoid each other from now on."

"You sound very sure of yourself."

She recalled the bleak look on Mr. Murray's normally cheerful face. "Earlier, in the hall, I'm afraid he might have overheard my sister voicing some rather unflattering opinions."

Ned's brows lifted. "Dare I ask?"

They strolled side by side out of the yard and along the wide path that ran parallel to the woods bordering Appersett House. The ground was covered in a light dusting of new-fallen snow. It melted into slush beneath the worn soles of Sophie's half boots.

"If you must know," she said, "it was something about his being in trade."

"Ah." Ned's deep voice was peculiarly neutral.

"I don't share her opinions."

"Your parents do."

Sophie didn't care for his blunt assertion, but she didn't argue with it. He was right, after all. There was no good reason to deny it. "My parents aren't unique among their class."

"And yet they've pressed you to accept me, a man whose entire fortune is built on trade." He looked at her. "Are you to be the sacrifice by which they maintain their place in society?"

She winced. "That's rather harsh."

"You said they used your dowry to have Appersett House fitted for gas."

Heat rose up in her face. "So they did."

"A singular decision."

"Only if you don't know my father." Sophie folded her arms at her waist. "When I was a girl, no more than thirteen, some gentlemen from the railway company came to Milton St. Edmunds. They wanted to put a platform halt just outside the village. The villagers were against it. They couldn't abide the thought of railway tracks cutting across the countryside. But Papa knew we must have that station. He felt so strongly about it and argued so persuasively that all the villagers soon came around to his way of thinking. It was progress, you see. Just like the gaslight. And Papa has always said one can't stand in the way of progress."

Ned appeared unmoved by her tale. "Progress is all well and good. But just what did your father expect you to do for a husband?"

"My parents expected both my sister and me to marry well. That's why they brought us to London."

"One of you with a dowry and the other without."

She glanced at him as they walked, wondering what he was implying. "You make it sound as though a great injustice had been perpetrated against me."

"Hasn't there?"

"Not in the least. The plain fact is, I didn't wish to marry when I was nineteen, nor when I was twenty, nor one-and-twenty. My dowry meant nothing to me and everything to my father. Why shouldn't he have it if it would make him happy?"

"Did he ask you for it?"

"I beg your pardon?"

"Before he took it and used it on Appersett House, did he ask you if he could have it?"

Sophie didn't answer. Of course Papa hadn't asked her permission. Why would he? "Must we speak of such things?"

"Not if you object."

"I don't object. But I don't see how it will help us get to know each other any better. All it does is make me feel bad about myself."

Ned frowned. "Forgive me. That wasn't my intention."

She shrugged a shoulder. It wasn't a very ladylike gesture, but it was eloquent enough of her opinion on the matter. She didn't wish to discuss her dowry anymore. Nor did she wish to discuss the dratted gaslight.

"What would you like to talk about?" he asked.

She raised her head to look at the trees. The branches were frosted with snow. It sparkled like sugar in the morning sunlight. "It's beautiful when it's new, isn't it? So clean and white and perfect."

"It's certainly cleaner than it is in London."

"Does the snow get very dirty there? I imagine it must with all of the activity in the streets."

"Excessively so. Have you never seen it?"

She shook her head. "We've spent every winter here since I was born."

"Would you like to spend Christmas in London?" he asked. "To live there all the year round?"

Her stomach gave a nervous quiver. "I suppose it would be all right." They walked in silence for several steps. "Did you enjoy holidays in London when you were a boy?"

"I worked through most of them." Ned's mouth hitched into a fleeting smile at her expression. "You look appalled."

"Oh no," she stammered. "I just...I didn't realize..."

"All of my family worked. The shop was closed on Christmas Day, but there was always someone who needed something. My parents rarely turned people away. They were forever obliging their customers. It's a central tenet of their business."

"What sort of work did you do for them?"

"During the holidays? Deliveries, mostly. On Christmas Eve I used to take people their parcels. Last-minute Christmas gifts, most of them. Up one city street and down another, through the sleet and snow. It would get so I couldn't feel my hands."

"That's dreadful."

"It wasn't, actually. People were grateful for their parcels. They tipped rather generously. And then later, when my deliveries were finished and I returned to our apartments above the shop, my mother would give me a hot cup of tea and a biscuit. It was my reward for a job well done."

Sophie refrained from saying that a biscuit seemed a poor reward for a child forced to traipse through the sleet and snow on Christmas Eve. A child who was frozen through. Who couldn't even feel his hands. "Are you very close to your parents?"

"As much as they'll permit."

Her brow furrowed. "I don't understand. Don't they wish to be close with you?"

"My parents taught me the habits of hard work and economy. They also taught me self-denial, which I felt most keenly when they made me put by half my earnings each week. It was a hard lesson, but a good one. Because of them, I was able to save enough to make my first investment. It was a merchant ship sailing to the West Indies. Murray and I each put all our savings into its cargo. Had the ship been lost at sea, we'd have been ruined. Instead, it arrived safely back in port, making us very rich indeed." He looked at her briefly. "You might say that everything I have I owe to my parents. But they're not warm people, for all that. They're not given to an excess of emotion."

She cast him a sidelong glance. His expression was as solemn as ever, but his black hair was rumpled, a section near the front standing half on end. It was oddly endearing. On every other occasion she'd been with him, his hair had been combed into meticulous order. There had never been a strand out of place. She decided she preferred it this way. He looked far less intimidating. As if he'd just risen from his bed in the morning.

The thought brought another flush of heat to her face. She swiftly looked away from him, pretending to be absorbed in admiring the snow-covered landscape. "Do you consider yourself to be a warm person?"

"Compared to my parents?"

"Compared to anyone."

Ned didn't answer right away. When he did, he spoke with a greater than usual degree of care. "I'm not a man given to great expressions of emotion. It's not how I was raised. It's not how I've lived my life. But I do feel things deeply. I may not always show it, but I do."

She stopped beneath one of the trees that stood at the edge of the path. Its wide branches provided meager shelter against a sudden flurry of snow. "I was afraid you were made of stone. Until the day I came to your office, I thought you might be."

"I wasn't very warm to you then."

"No, but it was then I realized..." She backed up against the tree trunk as he came to stand in front of her. He was so tall and darkly handsome; his blue eyes fixed on her with a single-mindedness that made her pulse tremble.

How many ladies before her had been the beneficiaries of that intent blue stare? How many had held Edward Sharpe riveted?

A wave of shyness assailed her. She was no experienced London flirt. She couldn't act the coquette to save her life.

"What did you realize?" he asked.

"That I'd hurt you somehow. Until that day, I hadn't thought you capable of being hurt. I didn't think you cared about me one way or another."

"A foolish assumption."

"Based on the evidence of my eyes and ears."

He set a gloved hand on a branch beside her, dislodging another fall of snow. "It worked both ways, you know."

"What did?"

"The lack of communication between us."

"I communicated," she said. "It was you who was always silent and brooding."

"You did talk to me, I'll give you that." His eyes flickered with rare humor. "You had a great deal to say about the weather."

A smile threatened. She barely succeeded in suppressing it. "It's a perfectly acceptable subject."

"And a very boring one." Ned loomed over her, his arm caging her against the tree. "The snow is very white and very beautiful," he said in a primly accented monotone. "The sky is very blue and the sun is very bright."

She bit her lip to keep from laughing. "That's not how I sound!"

"No. When you're voicing atmospheric platitudes, you sound a great deal prettier. I believe I could listen to you talk about the weather all day."

"Good," she said tartly. "Because I intend to rhapsodize about the snow all through Christmas."

"Heaven help me."

She did smile then. And he smiled back at her, holding her gaze. Her heart performed a queer little somersault. How his face changed when he smiled! There was a sparkle in his eyes and a flash of strong white teeth. A brilliance to make her catch her breath.

"Had I known teasing would make you smile so brightly, I'd have done it sooner," he said.

"I'm sure I've smiled at you before."

"Not like this you haven't."

"I'm merely surprised," she said. "It's not like you to engage in light-hearted banter."

"I don't claim to be an expert at it. I'm certainly not up to Murray's weight."

"Thank goodness for that."

Ned's mouth hitched. "Perhaps I should take another leaf out of Murray's book."

"What do you mean?"

"Court you as I would someone of my own class. As I would have courted a stonemason's daughter."

Sophie didn't know whether to be intrigued or appalled. A flood of questions filled her head. She didn't know which one to ask him first. "Is it really so different?"

"In some ways, I expect. There are still rules—an abundance of them—but a fellow can be a bit easier. He can tease and flirt. Steal a kiss, perhaps."

Her heart executed another acrobatic gyration. She couldn't imagine Edward Sharpe teasing and flirting with anyone, least of all her. As for stealing a kiss…

"Would you have kissed me if I was a stonemason's daughter?" The question tumbled out in an anxious rush of breath.

Ned's gaze darkened. He took another step toward her, a flash of something in his blue eyes that was almost predatory. "Would you have liked me to kiss you?"

She pressed her back to the tree trunk. The dusting of snowflakes clinging to the bark melted into the fabric of her paletot. "I…I don't know. Perhaps. If we grew fond of each other."

"In other words, you'd have preferred I refrain."

"Well," she said with sudden frankness, "I don't think I'd have enjoyed it if you'd simply grabbed me and kissed me. A lady likes to prepare herself for such an event."

"Fair enough. Are the next nine days enough time to prepare yourself? Because, unless you very strenuously object, I intend to kiss you this Christmas."

Sophie stared at him, her mouth suddenly dry. It took all of her strength of will to compose herself. To moisten her lips and formulate words more substantial than a breathless squeak. "Under the mistletoe, I presume."

"Under the mistletoe. Under the gaslight. Under the stars." Ned bent his head close to hers. "Perhaps all three."

SEVEN

The rest of the day progressed in a haphazard fashion. After washing and changing his clothes, Ned proceeded downstairs to the breakfast parlor. Eggs, sausages, and other hot foods were arrayed in silver serving dishes on a mahogany sideboard. He fetched a plate and helped himself to a generous portion of each before joining the other guests at the table.

Sir William was seated at the head of it, perusing a newspaper while a footman poured his coffee. Walter was there as well, as was the vicar, Mr. Hubbard, and a reedy-looking fellow who Ned understood to be the village schoolmaster. Another of Sophie's last-minute guests, he suspected. And, if Sir William's scowl was any indication, not one who was very welcome.

They were joined in short order by Ned's father and a few more of the guests, a smattering of gentlemen and unmarried ladies. The married ladies, including Lady Appersett and Ned's mother, didn't make an appearance at all. They had the privilege of having breakfast delivered to them in bed.

Ned didn't see Sophie at the table. Instead, he found himself seated between Walter and the vicar's widowed sister, Mrs.

Lanyon, who—like her brother—had a great deal to say on the subject of Prince Albert's death.

"The Queen's grief can scarcely be imagined," she confided to Ned in sepulchral tones. "To lose a much-loved spouse—to see him struck down in the very prime of his life—such pain and desolation cannot be measured—"

"I say, Sharpe," Sir William interrupted. "Do you ride?"

Ned lowered his fork to his plate. "I do, sir."

"Capital, capital." Sir William finished off his coffee and rose from his seat. "Meet me at the stables in half an hour. I'll take you down to see some of the improvements."

Ned watched him leave, frowning. He was well aware that Sir William expected him to help the estate in some way. But what form that help would take had never been discussed. Ned had assumed it would consist of settling Sir William's debts or the equivalent. A small price to pay for the privilege of marrying the man's daughter.

Not that Sophie was ready to marry him. Hell, she wasn't even ready to let him kiss her.

But she'd smiled at him.

And her voice had quavered when she spoke.

It was progress, Ned decided as he finished his coffee. And the day wasn't half over yet.

"Going riding with Sir William?" Walter murmured. "Quite an honor."

"Jealous?"

"Hardly."

Ned gave his friend a searching look. He was more rumpled than usual, his eyes lacking their normal twinkle of good cheer. "Miss Appersett told me what happened this morning."

"Of course she did."

"You're not...*upset* about it, are you?"

Walter gave a dismissive snort. "God, no." He speared a piece of sausage with his fork. "What difference does it make to me?"

Ned's gaze remained on him until Mrs. Lanyon once again commanded his attention. When she paused to draw breath, he rose and made his excuses. He didn't know where the devil Sophie had got to, nor where her shrewish little sister was, but he didn't have a second to linger. Not if he was to be on time for his meeting with their father.

Sophie sank down on the cushioned window seat beside her sister. The chintz curtains had been pulled back to reveal a view of the snow-covered north lawn. It wasn't a heavy snowfall as yet. Certainly not deep enough for them to bring out the sleds or hitch up the sleighs. But Sophie had hopes for tomorrow. The temperature would surely drop by several more degrees, ensuring a deep enough blanket of snow for all their Christmas activities.

Until then, she must contrive other ways to keep the guests busy. There would be music and games, naturally. And Mrs. Phillips had already started the baking. By this time tomorrow, the house would smell of fresh-cut pine, hot gingerbread, baked apples, and peppermint. Sophie could hardly wait.

If only Emily would allow herself to get into the holiday spirit. The poor dear. Sophie had never seen her so morose. Not even when she was pouting over being denied a favorite treat.

"I didn't know he was standing there," she said once again. "If I had known…"

"Yes, it's very unfortunate," Sophie acknowledged. "But don't you see? It doesn't matter whether he was there or not. You shouldn't say such unkind things about people."

"It's nothing worse than what Papa says."

"Papa is from a different generation. He's old and set in his ways. But you and I…" Sophie tipped her sister's chin up with her fingers, forcing her to meet her eyes. "We're part of the modern age, my dear. Everything is changing so very rapidly. We must change along with it or be left behind in the dust. Like the dinosaurs we saw at the Great Exhibition. Do you remember?"

Emily's eyes puddled with tears. She sniffed loudly. "I don't want to be a dinosaur."

"Then take this as a lesson. We mustn't be so judgmental. And we must never say things behind a person's back that we wouldn't say to their face." Sophie let go of her sister's chin and reached into the pocket of her morning dress to retrieve a handkerchief. "Here. Blow your nose. There's no point crying. You'll only upset Mama."

"I'm not crying." Emily blotted her eyes. "And I wouldn't upset Mama for the world."

"I'm glad to hear it. Are you ready to get dressed now? Or do you need me to stay a little longer?"

Emily was still in her wrapper, her sable hair a mass of tangles down her back. She crumpled the soggy handkerchief in her hand. "What about Mr. Murray? I'll have to see him again. And I know he hates me."

"I doubt that very much," Sophie said. "And even if he does harbor some ill will, does it truly matter so much what he thinks?"

"No. But I wish him to like me all the same."

"He's practically a stranger, Emmy."

"Not entirely."

"No?" Sophie's brows lifted in surprise.

"We first met the day I was allowed to accompany you to Cremorne Gardens to see the high-wire act."

"I know that much." Sophie had gone with Mr. Sharpe and a small party of friends, Mr. Murray among them. Emily had not initially been invited but, at the last moment, she'd insisted on coming. Sophie hadn't minded. The outing had seemed a harmless enough treat to share with her sister.

"We met again the next week at Mrs. Ashburnham's dinner party."

"I'd forgotten that," Sophie said. "You were seated beside him, weren't you?"

Emily nodded. "He teased me and made me laugh. He was so absurd."

"He's a good-humored gentleman."

"I thought so." Emily's eyes dropped to her handkerchief. "A week later, I encountered him at Hatchard's. He retrieved a book for me off a shelf that was too high."

Sophie refrained from commenting. She knew only too well how such inconsequential actions could come to loom large in the imagination of a romantic-minded young lady. Hadn't she just spent a good half hour reliving her walk with Ned? Analyzing his every action and dissecting his every word?

"I thought I would see him again when you went to Fleet Street," Emily confessed.

"Ah. So that's why you wished to come."

"Yes, but…when I saw how dark and dirty the street was—and how ugly his offices—I knew I'd made a mistake. He's a tradesman. A stonemason's son, Papa says." Tears sprang once more into Emily's eyes. "And now he despises me."

"Perhaps you might apologize to him?" Sophie suggested.

"Why?" Emily snuffled into her handkerchief. "Everything I said was true. I can't be sorry for it. I'm only sorry that he heard me. I didn't intend to hurt his feelings."

"Oh, Emmy." Sophie sighed. "You have a great deal of growing up to do."

Her sister made no reply. She was staring out the window. Sophie followed her gaze. There were two gentleman riding down the snowy path, one on a chestnut hunter and the other on a strapping gray. It was Papa and—

Good gracious!

"Is that Mr. Sharpe?" Emily asked.

"I fear it is."

"Where's Papa taking him?"

There was a sinking feeling in Sophie's stomach. "To see the gas works, I suspect."

Emily wrinkled her nose. "Dirty, smelly place. If Papa ever spends my dowry, I hope he'll use it for something more pleasing. An orangery, or a tennis court, perhaps."

Sophie rose, only half listening. "I'll send Annie to help you dress," she said as she turned to leave.

After exiting Emily's bedroom, Sophie went to her own. She briefly considered changing into a riding habit, having her mare saddled, and setting off after Papa and Ned. But that would be overreacting, surely. Besides, Ned was more than capable of withstanding any pressure Papa put to bear. At least, Sophie hoped he was.

Sir William was a man who was fond of good horseflesh. He kept a string of hunters along with his riding horses. Big, leanly-muscled beasts with near-perfect conformation. The one he'd assigned to Ned was a well-built gray with a great deal of spirit. Ned supposed it was a challenge of sorts. A test to see whether or not he could control a mount that wasn't lame in all four legs.

As a humbly born Londoner, he hadn't been much of an equestrian in his youth. Riding horses were a luxury in the city, expensive to buy and to maintain. It wasn't until he was an adult that he'd learned to ride properly.

He didn't enjoy it overmuch. Not as much as Sir William, certainly. But he was more than equipped to handle the mood swings of the handsome gray, even when the bad-tempered blackguard set his teeth on the bit and refused to let it go.

"Progress," Sir William said proudly as they rode away from Appersett House's private gas works. The ground was white with fresh-fallen snow. "That's what that is, Sharpe. A modern marvel of engineering."

"It's none too healthy for the workers."

"Nonsense! I'll have you know that my gas works is cleaner and better run than the gas works in the city. The men can breathe without inhaling poison."

Ned wasn't so sure. During his brief tour, he'd inhaled enough noxious fumes to bring on a headache.

Not that he was unappreciative of the innovation. A country house gas works was a rarity. Rarer still, the elegance and efficiency of the one he'd just encountered. It was made of stone, with bricked archways and chimneys. A skeleton crew of soot-covered workmen were employed within to shovel coal into sealed retorts, which were heated by a large furnace. The crude gas produced was then condensed and purified before being pumped to the main house via a series of underground pipes.

The process was time-consuming and the smell particularly foul. But it was an impressive business for all that. Truly a product of the modern age.

Ned brought his horse up alongside his host. Softly falling snowflakes gathered on the brim of his hat and melted into his horse's mane. It was getting colder by the minute. "It must have been quite an expense." Upwards of five thousand pounds, unless he was mistaken. A hefty sum, even for a gentleman who was well-to-do.

He wondered how much of that amount had been Sophie's dowry.

"I won't be so vulgar as to discuss the cost," Sir William said. "Except to say that it was worth every penny."

"You haven't any regrets?"

"Bah! What is there to regret? Appersett House has a reputation to uphold. My lady wife would've rather had the drawing room repapered or the carpets replaced. What's unique in that, I ask you? But gaslight. Oho!" He practically crowed. "How many other estates in the country are fitted for gas, sir? Appersett House is unique among its kind. And when I've finished the next phase of modernizations—"

Ned looked at him sharply. "The *next* phase?"

"Plumbing, my good man. By this time next year, we'll have tiled bathing rooms and water closets, shower baths and sinks with hot and cold running water. Just think of it!"

Ned thought of the expense. Was *he* meant to subsidize it? Or was Sir William expecting a windfall of some sort?

Ned saw no reason to beat about the bush. "These are costly improvements for a man in your position."

Sir William's body went rigid in the saddle. "My position?" His horse commenced an agitated dance. "And just what is my position, sir?"

"You mentioned having lost your daughter's dowry on speculation."

"Eh?" Sir William attempted to calm his mount. "Ah, yes. Speculation. Quite right. I don't advise it, Sharpe. One shouldn't gamble."

"I never do, sir," Ned said gravely. "I'm exceedingly careful with my money."

"A common philosophy among men of your class. Counting every shilling. But you're not a poor man now. If you were, I'd never permit you within a mile of my daughter. She's a fine young lady. Far too elegant for a tradesman, as anyone can see."

"I won't dispute that."

"And whoever is fortunate enough to marry my daughters may one day have Appersett House. The jewel in the crown, some might say. A prize more valuable than a mere wife. I've yet to decide who I'll leave it to."

"It's unentailed?" Ned couldn't conceal his surprise. "I thought—"

"That it would go to some nephew or second cousin or other? Poppycock. Do you think I'd modernize my estate merely to hand it over to an insignificant twig on the Appersett family tree? Not on your life, sir. My father and grandfather executed a deed of disentailment decades ago. Needed to sell off some of the land, more's the pity."

"But if it's unentailed, it could be sold to pay your debts. Don't you realize the risk—"

"Appersett House sold?" Sir William gave a booming laugh. "The idea of it!"

Ned stared at the man in disbelief. Didn't he understand the danger in which he placed his family? The risk inherent in these endless improvements and modernizations?

His horse stamped beneath him in impatience. Ned loosened the reins. The stable was in sight and both horses were anxious to get back to it.

A stable lad met them in the yard. Ned dismounted and handed him his horse. Sir William did the same, pausing to bark instructions.

Ned was obliged to wait for his host, though he didn't feel much like doing so. He needed a moment alone. Time to think. Better yet, he needed another moment with Sophie. She was the whole point of this visit. The entire reason he was even considering subsidizing Sir William's latest scheme.

"I have the plans in my study," Sir William said as they walked back to the house. "An architect in London has drawn them up for me. He's keen to start work." He glanced at Ned, his eyes hard as flint. "Come by after you've changed. We can discuss the estimates."

EIGHT

The attics at Appersett House were a vast honeycomb of hidden spaces filled with ramshackle crates, leather trunks, and Holland-covered furnishings from generations past. There was no exact order to the way things were stored. A painting with torn canvas here, a faded tapestry there. Sophie peered under quite a few sheets before finding what she was looking for.

The family's Christmas decorations resided in three enormous trunks. As she swept away the covers, the dust stirred up in a cloud. She sneezed mightily.

"Bless you," a deep male voice said.

Sophie whipped around with a start. Ned was standing at the entry to the attic, one shoulder propped against the doorjamb. He looked as solemn and self-possessed as he had while courting her in London. A tall, darkly serious man with an unfathomable expression. A far cry from the smiling fellow who'd promised to kiss her under the mistletoe.

But not just under the mistletoe.

Under the gaslight, he'd said. And under the stars.

Her heartbeat quickened. "What are *you* doing here?"

Ned ducked inside, shutting the door behind him. "Looking for you."

"You shouldn't be here."

"Why? Is the attic off-limits for guests? Your mother never said so."

"My mother?"

"Who do you think told me where to find you?"

Sophie dusted off her hands. "No. It's not off-limits. But we shouldn't be here alone together, as well you know."

Ned crossed the attic floor, navigating carefully around the clutter. "We'll have to keep it a secret, then."

"There are no such things as secrets at country house parties. Haven't you heard?"

His lips quirked. "Point taken."

For a moment, she was tempted to smile. To try and recapture a little of the magic of their morning walk in the snow. But her nerves wouldn't permit it. The image of him riding off with her father was seared on her brain. "Where have you been all day?"

"Where have *you* been?" he countered. "You weren't at breakfast."

"There was a small crisis with my sister. By the time I came downstairs you were already gone."

"Your father invited me to go riding."

"Yes, I saw the pair of you from Emily's window." She regarded him with a worried frown. "Is everything all right?"

"With your father?" Ned shrugged. "It's fine. He was very civil. He took me to see the gas works."

"I thought as much." Sophie continued to look at him, unable to quell a rising sense of dread. "You were gone a long while."

Ned seemed to hesitate. "Your father wished to speak with me in his study when we returned."

"What about?"

"Nothing that concerns you."

Sophie huffed. "What a thoroughly patronizing thing to say." She turned back to the trunks. There were only two things Papa could wish to speak to Ned about. One of them was her. The other was money.

"What have you there?" Ned asked, coming closer. "Are those your Christmas decorations?"

"They're half full of rubbish, I expect. I'll have to go through them."

"I'll help you, if you like."

"Please yourself." She knelt in front of the largest trunk. Her skirts billowed out around her over a sea of petticoats and crinoline. It left little room for Ned. He didn't seem to mind. He sank down atop one of the trunks at her side. The toes of his leather boots slid beneath the hemline of her skirts.

Heat crept up Sophie's throat.

He rested an arm across his knees. "Are you going to open it?"

"Of course." She unfastened the metal latch and pushed back the lid. Within were a carelessly packed jumble of holiday artifacts. She scanned the contents. "This must be the wrong trunk."

"Aren't those Christmas decorations?"

"They are, but what we want are the ribbons and tinsel. There are foil stars, too. At least, there should be. If not in these trunks, then somewhere else."

Ned leaned forward. "What's that?"

"This?" Sophie withdrew a partially wrapped porcelain figure. She held it up for Ned's perusal. "One of the shepherds from our old Nativity set."

"That must be worth salvaging."

"No." She looked at the chipped figurine, remembering the last Christmas it had been displayed. It was more than ten years ago. A veritable lifetime. "We haven't used it in ages."

"Why not?"

"The set is incomplete." She paused before adding, "Papa lost his temper one year and smashed the baby Jesus to smithereens. Emily wanted to place an egg in the manger instead, but Mama said it would be sacrilegious. She wrapped up the remaining pieces and packed them away. We never speak of it now."

Ned looked mildly scandalized. "Why in the world would your father destroy the baby Jesus?"

Sophie placed the porcelain shepherd back in the trunk and closed the lid. She turned to look at Ned. "When I was twelve, my mother and father had another child. A little boy. He lived but one day. There were difficulties. Indeed, we were fortunate not to lose my mother as well. The doctor said there would be no more children."

Ned's brow creased with understanding. "I'm sorry. I didn't know."

"He would have been my father's heir. When he died… Papa was grieved, but he was also quite angry. He raged at everyone." She reached to open the next trunk, her fingers hesitating over the latch. "Do you think sons are more valuable than daughters?"

"Not to me they wouldn't be."

She gave a slight smile. "That's easy to say now, but what if all you had were daughters?"

"I would thank God for them."

"Would you?"

Ned's expression turned grave. "My parents lost several children before I arrived. Most of them lived no longer than your brother. Healthy children are a miracle, whatever their sex. One must be grateful for them."

She stared at him for a long moment. "How little I know of you."

"There's not a great deal worth knowing. Not by society's standards."

"Isn't there?"

"I have neither birth nor breeding. I never attended Oxford or Cambridge. I've never toured the capitals of Europe or met the Queen. Some might argue that I'm not even a gentleman." His blue eyes were as solemn as ever. "I'm just a man, Sophie."

"No ordinary man could have made of his life what you have. Not if he'd started where you did."

"That was only ambition and a bit of luck."

"I think it must have taken very hard work," she said.

He smiled. "That, too."

Her lips tilted upward, returning his smile briefly before she opened the lid of the next trunk. Inside were crumpled newspapers and a few brittle remnants of dried-out greenery. She cleared them away, revealing the shimmer of silver foil and gold tinsel beneath.

"Is that what you were looking for?" Ned asked.

"Yes, precisely." She rummaged around. "But the ribbons aren't here. They must be in that one."

Ned stood and opened the trunk he'd been using as a makeshift seat. A wild tangle of red and green velvet ribbons sprang up from within. He attempted to lift one of them out, but it was inextricably knotted to its brethren.

"Oh dear." Sophie bit her lip. "What a dreadful tangle."

"Do you still want them?"

"Yes." She moved to rise. Ned reached out his hands to assist her. She took them gratefully, allowing him to draw her to her feet. It was the first time their bare hands had met. There was a warmth to it. An intimacy that made her stomach quiver. As if a hundred butterflies had just fluttered their wings. Did he feel it as keenly as she did?

"Thank you," she said. "I'm afraid I've gone stiff from kneeling on the floor."

"And collected all the dust from it besides."

"Have I? What a nuisance."

He gazed down at her, his large hands still engulfing hers. "I'll carry those trunks down for you, shall I?"

"You needn't. We can just as easily summon a footman."

"I'm happy to do it." He gave her hands a gentle squeeze before releasing her. "We'll need to get started disentangling those ribbons."

Sophie brushed off her skirts. "We can leave them with the older ladies and gentlemen while the rest of us go out to gather greenery tomorrow. It will give them something to do."

"You don't include the older guests?"

"In cutting down greenery and dragging back the Yule log? Everyone is welcome, naturally, but there are always a few who'd rather stay behind. Some of them can't abide dampness and chills."

"My own mother for one."

"And mine," Sophie said. "They wouldn't get much enjoyment tramping about in the snow, searching for mistletoe."

"Does mistletoe grow hereabouts?" Ned asked.

She nodded. "Far out in the woods."

"You'll have to show me," he said softly.

Her heart thumped hard. "If you like."

NINE

Ned thrust his hands into the pockets of his heavy woolen coat as he walked along with the rest of the guests who'd chosen to brave the elements. There were about twenty of them altogether, not counting the servants. All bundled up in coats and scarves and fur-trimmed cloaks as they made their way out into the woods behind Appersett House.

The weather had grown chillier overnight. He'd been awakened by an icy draft seeping in through the chimney. The windows of the guest bedroom he occupied had been covered with frost. When he'd peered out through the encrusted glass, he'd scarcely been able to see for the snowfall. It was a blur of white, not only falling but whipping round in little flurries

It had calmed by midmorning, permitting them all to venture out to gather greenery. Even so, the remnants of that tiny blizzard were visible everywhere.

The landscape was blanketed in a pristine layer of snow. It covered the paths, cloaked the shrubbery, and disposed itself in sparkling heaps on the branches of the trees. So much snow glittered in the weak sunlight it almost hurt his eyes to look at it.

It wasn't unduly cold for all that. At least, Ned didn't think so. His blood was pumping hot in his veins at the prospect of spending more time with Sophie.

He was making progress with her at last. Little by little, he was somehow managing to talk to her. To share something of himself. Of his history. That was what she wanted, wasn't it? For him to open up to her? To show her who he really was?

It was the complete opposite of what the *Gentlemen's Book of Etiquette* advised.

According to the chapter on polite conversation, a gentleman was never to discuss business with a lady he was courting. He wasn't to overwhelm her with the tedious details of his professional life. Nor was he to sink into low conversation about personal matters.

Ned wasn't entirely sure what qualified as low conversation, but he suspected that matters of finance would be at the top of the list. Money, it seemed, was only a suitable topic when speaking with a lady's father.

As for what was appropriate to discuss with the lady herself, the book was rather vague.

Rule No. 25: Let your conversation with a lady be dictated by sound sense, and on the common topics of everyday occurrence.

The weather, in other words.

It was not his favorite subject at the moment. Not that it mattered. As they trudged through the woods, there was little prospect for private conversation.

Sophie was busy playing hostess. She'd gathered a cluster of ladies around her, including her sister, three of her sister's very silly friends, the village schoolmaster's wife, a rather toplofty viscountess, and two highly eligible society misses who Ned recognized from the London season. They giggled and talked over each other and intermittently broke into a discordant verse from a Christmas carol.

The remaining gentlemen were making just as much noise. The sight of so much snow had raised their holiday spirits to an irritating degree. They joined the ladies in talking, laughing, and carol singing.

Ned cast a glance back at Walter. In other circumstances, he'd have been one of the first to add his voice to the cacophony. Today, however, he didn't seem to feel much like talking, let alone singing.

Ned drew back from the group to walk alongside him. Unless he was mistaken, his friend was still very much in the doldrums.

"Mark my words, Ned," he grumbled, "we'll end up cutting and hauling the Yule log ourselves. None of those fine gentlemen look strong enough to fell a sapling."

"Are you complaining?"

"Just stating a fact."

"Still in a mood, I take it."

Walter exhaled. "She apologized to me. Can you believe it?"

"Who did?"

"Emily Appersett. Last night after dinner. I was making my escape to the billiard room and she cornered me in the hall."

Ned grimaced. He didn't think much of Sophie's sister. She was spoiled and self-indulgent. And she commanded far too much of Sophie's precious time. "You need to stay away from her."

"You think I don't know that?"

"Knowing and doing are two different things. You're my friend and my business partner. If you meddle with her, I'm the one who'll have to answer for it."

"God forbid I should cause you a moment's inconvenience," Walter said acidly. And then: "I have no intention of meddling with her."

"Good."

They walked in silence for several steps before Walter heaved a heavy sigh. His cold breath was a visible puff in the frosty December air. "What you see in this family, I can't begin to imagine."

"I don't care about the family. It's Miss Appersett I'm after."

"You can't have one without the other."

Ned looked straight ahead, his jaw set. "Watch me."

"Mr. Sharpe!" Mr. Hubbard, the vicar, called back to them. "Mr. Murray! Do join us. Mr. Fortescue and I have been having the most stimulating discussion about last Sunday's sermon. Are you familiar with ancient Aramaic?"

Mr. Fortescue, the schoolmaster, gave them both a nervous glance.

Ned felt the sudden urge to laugh. Ancient Aramaic? Good God.

"I don't know about Sharpe," Walter said, "but I don't speak a word of it."

They were spared from further conversation by Mrs. Fortescue and one of the young ladies from London. Miss Tunstall? Or was it Miss Trowbridge? Ned couldn't remember.

"No more ancient Aramaic, Vicar," she said. "Today is for caroling and mistletoe."

"Indeed," Mrs. Fortescue agreed, linking her arm through her husband's. "If you must argue about the Bible, let it be over the Christmas story."

"The English translation, if you please," Walter said. They all laughed.

Up ahead, the rest of their party had stopped in the midst of a grove of pine trees. Ned and the other stragglers joined them.

"Break off as many boughs as you can," Sophie was saying to the gentlemen. "We ladies will drag them back to the house."

Ned watched her issuing orders. Her cheeks were flushed from the cold, her brown eyes shining. Christmas agreed with her. So did Appersett House, he was obliged to admit. The grandeur of it. The luxurious furnishings and rich surfaces. The sense of history about it all.

He wondered if she could ever find happiness in London. If she could ever be content as the wife of a tradesman. A mere draper's son.

"What about the mistletoe, Miss Appersett?" one of the younger ladies called out with a giggle.

"We can sometimes find it growing on the oak trees," Sophie said. "They're on the opposite side of the estate. Shall we split up?"

It was soon decided that Walter, Emily, and Mr. Fortescue and his wife would stay with half the group collecting pine boughs while the other half of the group, comprised of Sophie, Ned, Mr. Hubbard, and the younger guests, would strike out to find the mistletoe.

Ned was content to let the young people run ahead with the vicar while he fell into step beside Sophie. She glanced up at him.

"We're among the elders of the party, I'm afraid," she said. "Reduced to chaperonage."

"The vicar and I, perhaps," Ned conceded. "But you? You're hardly in your dotage."

"I'm three and twenty. It's not exactly the first bloom of youth."

"You know my opinions on the matter."

She bent her head, smiling. "Yes. You find me a beautiful creature."

Ned inwardly winced. As compliments went, he saw no fault with it, but clearly Sophie found it lacking somehow. "That offends you."

"No," she said. "It doesn't offend me. It's a very nice thing to say."

"Then why do I get the impression you'd rather I'd never said it?"

Sophie cast him another glance. "Beauty doesn't last forever. Not the exterior kind. If that's what you value in me, you'll soon be disappointed."

"I didn't ask leave to court you merely for your beauty. I thought I made that clear the night you came to my office."

Her smile faded. "Yes. You were very kind."

"It wasn't kindness. It was the truth." He'd wanted her from the first. Had known as soon as he looked at her that she was someone worth having in his life, no matter the cost.

It hadn't been love at first sight. That was too trite. Too simplistic. But something within him had recognized something in her. Had understood that she would be important to him.

In business, he'd learned to trust his instincts. He'd seen no reason to doubt them when it came to matters of courtship and marriage.

"The truth is in rather short supply in my life," she said. "You'll forgive me for doubting it when I hear it."

Ned caught her gently by the arm and turned her to face him. The rest of the group had drifted ahead, leaving them standing alone under the snow-covered boughs of an enormous pine tree. He looked her very steadily in the eye. "I won't ever lie to you, Sophie."

Beneath the ribbon tie of her wool cloak, her throat spasmed in a visible swallow. "Won't you?"

"Never."

"Then tell me what you and my father talked about yesterday in his study."

Ned's hand fell from her arm. He shook his head, amazed at his own stupidity. "I walked very neatly into that, didn't I?"

"It's not a trap. All you need do is tell me what he wanted of you."

"I already told you it wasn't important."

"No. What you said was that it didn't concern me. Which is absolute flummery and you know it."

"It doesn't matter."

"It matters to *me*. I won't be haggled over in secret, smoke-filled rooms. Even dairy cows are negotiated for in the open-air market."

He choked on a laugh. Or maybe it was a groan. "A dairy cow? That's hardly flattering to either of us."

"Given the circumstances, I find it a rather apt comparison."

"It's a ridiculous comparison."

"You're determined to patronize me," she said. "To treat me like a child who has no say in her own life. In her own future. I see how it is now."

Ned sighed. "My dear girl, doesn't it occur to you that I'm trying to spare you a burden?"

"Why should you? I've been shouldering the burdens of my family for as long as I can remember. I shan't crumple like a leaf to hear that my father has a new scheme for improving the estate." Her eyes flashed. "Aha! That's it, isn't it? He wishes to re-gravel the drive or—"

"It's not the drive."

"What, then?"

He ran a hand over his hair. "It's the plumbing."

"The *plumbing*?"

Ned grimaced. "Not the most decorous subject to discuss with a lady." Indeed, he wondered what the author of *The Gentlemen's Book of Etiquette* would have to say about it.

Sophie fell silent for a long moment. A shadow of worry darkened her brow. "I never thought... That is, he's mentioned bathing rooms and shower baths and the like, but the cost of such a project could never be borne. The gaslight has already nearly forced us into penury. Another improvement on that scale would be the end of us."

"I'm not a pauper, Sophie."

"No, but...we don't even know if we suit each other. Or what might happen after Christmas." She resumed walking, her pace quickening with every step. "You should leave Derbyshire. You should run far and fast from my family."

Ned caught up with her easily.

"The plumbing won't be enough," she said. "You must realize that. It will no more satisfy him than the gaslight or the platform halt."

"I thought you approved of progress?"

"Yes. I—" She faltered. "I do approve. I try to, anyway. But this? It's too much, Ned. When Mama finds out—"

"Is it only the money you object to?"

"*Only* the money, you say. As if money is a small concern. And even if it weren't. I'm not worth half the sum."

"And you accuse me of talking flummery?"

"It's not flummery. It's reality. I'm doing you the courtesy of being honest."

"Permit me to do the same." Ned caught her by the arm once again, obliging her to stop and look at him. His voice was low and fierce. "You say you know nothing about me. That you don't know if you like me or not. Or whether we suit or not. But during those two months I courted you in London, I learned to like you very much. I watched you and listened to you. I saw how gracious you are. How kind and sweet and warm. How very much a lady. I don't need the next eight days to determine how I feel about you. I already know how I feel. I admire you, Sophie. I want you for my own. If I have to modernize your father's estate into the next millennium, it would be a small price to pay for the privilege of having you."

Sophie gaze held his, a look of muted astonishment on her face. As if she were stunned by his words and trying very hard not to show it.

And then, just like that, her mouth trembled.

"You're wrong," she said. "I do like you. I like when you talk to me—and when you held my hands in the attic. I like that you don't wish to lay a burden on me." Her eyes glistened with tears. "I'm being silly and stupid."

"No," he said softly. "You're not."

She brushed a gloved hand over her cheek. "Only yesterday I was wishing my sister would have some holiday cheer, and here I am like any watering pot. I beg your pardon, Ned."

His heart turned over. He wanted to take her in his arms. Promise her the world, if only...

But it was too soon. And she was upset. Overwhelmed. He'd had no idea her father's profligacy had affected her so much. Only a cad would take advantage.

"I want you to do something for me," he said. "For the next eight days, I want you to let me shoulder this burden."

She shook her head. "It's not yours to bear."

"Consider it a Christmas gift." She began to object, but he anticipated her. "You needn't fear that I'll infer some kind of promise or commitment from it. What happens after the holidays is still entirely your choice. But while I'm here in Derbyshire, let me worry about your father's ambitions for the estate. You can concern yourself with more important things."

"Such as?"

"Good Lord, I don't know. Decorating? Singing carols? Gathering mistletoe?" He looked in the direction that the others had gone. "Speaking of which, we seem to have become separated from our party."

Sophie followed his gaze. "So much for our faithful chaperonage."

"Let's hope the vicar is doing a better job of it."

"Shall we try and find them?" she asked.

"If you like," he said. "Or we could search out some mistletoe for ourselves."

Her cheeks were already flushed from the cold, but he could have sworn they turned a little redder. "There was some hereabouts last Christmas," she admitted. "Emily and I found it by the—"

Her words were interrupted by an ungodly shriek. They both turned in the direction from whence it came. Another high-pitched shriek heralded the arrival of one of the aristocratic young ladies they'd left behind to gather pine boughs. She ran toward them through the woods, her skirts clutched in her hands.

"Miss Appersett! Miss Appersett!" She came to a sliding halt in the snow in front of Sophie.

Sophie moved to steady her. "Miss Tunstall, what on earth is the matter?"

"It's your sister, ma'am," Miss Tunstall panted. "She's fallen on the ice and hurt her leg. She may have broken it. Or worse. Lady Barton mentioned amputation and Mr. Fortescue nearly fainted. Mrs. Fortescue said I was to fetch you straightaway."

Sophie's face drained of color. Ned moved to place a reassuring hand on her back. But she was already charging off, Miss Tunstall trotting at her side. "I must go to her," she said. "Tell the others—"

"Damn the others." Ned strode after her, ignoring Miss Tunstall's scandalized gasp. "Here. Take my arm. It won't help your sister if you injure yourself as well."

Sophie looked at him blankly for a moment. Then she nodded, seeming to bring her emotions under some semblance of control. "Yes. You're quite right." She took his arm, her fingers pressing tight into his sleeve as they retraced their steps back through the snow.

They'd gone no more than a few yards when they crossed paths with Walter Murray. He was carrying Emily Appersett in his arms.

"Not to worry," he said as he emerged from the woods. "Just a twisted ankle. She'll be fine once we get her back to the house."

"Oh, thank heaven." Sophie reached out to clasp her sister's hand. "My poor dear. Does it hurt terribly?"

Emily gave a weak smile. "It's better now."

Ned's gaze flicked from Emily's face to Walter's. His friend's foul mood appeared to have vanished. "How did it happen?"

"Overexuberance," Walter said. "A failing in the very young."

"I'm not so much younger than you," Emily retorted. "Not so anyone would notice."

"Whatever you say, brat." Walter adjusted his hold on her. "Tighten your arms around my neck, will you? I'd hate to drop you in a snowbank."

Emily clung to him fiercely. "You wouldn't dare."

Ned chanced a look at Sophie as they followed in Walter's wake. Her face was drawn with concern. Whatever was going on between Walter and her sister clearly didn't sit well with her. "It will be all right," he said quietly.

Sophie met his eyes. "I hope so, Ned. For everyone's sake."

TEN

The next two days passed in a blur of holiday revelry. While Emily rested on the sofa, a knitted blanket draped over her legs and her bandaged ankle elevated on a satin pillow, the rest of the party decorated the house with greenery, ribbons, and tinsel. The gentlemen hauled in the Yule log and the ladies gilded acorns and artificially frosted holly and ivy leaves with a mixture of alum and boiled water.

The following afternoon, Mrs. Sharpe joined them in the drawing room. She took a seat not far from Emily, her knitting needles soon clacking in a steady rhythm. "You'd be wise to stay off of it until the new year. Or risk walking with a limp for the rest of your days."

Emily looked doubtful. "That would mean missing the Christmas ball."

"A small price to pay to avoid permanent lameness."

"But I *must* dance, Mrs. Sharpe. It will be our first ball at Appersett House since the gaslight was installed. I wouldn't miss it for anything."

Sophie was seated at a low inlaid table with Miss Tunstall, the Viscountess Barton, and Mrs. Lanyon. She was mending the tree skirt while the other ladies worked together on the kissing bough. "Perhaps just one dance."

Emily snorted. "One? That's little better than nothing."

"How many waltzes will be played at the Christmas ball, Miss Appersett?" Miss Tunstall asked.

"Three or four, I should think," Sophie said.

Mrs. Sharpe's features tightened with disapproval.

Sophie didn't know why. It had been ages since the waltz was considered scandalous. Then again, Ned's mother was a woman of advanced years. "Do you object to waltzing, ma'am?"

"I object to public displays, in any form," Mrs. Sharpe said with a forceful click of her needles. "Waltzing is but another excuse for excessive intimacy between young men and women. It can lead to nothing but trouble."

Emily struggled up to a sitting position on the sofa. "But everyone waltzes at balls."

"It's true," Sophie said. "It's unexceptionable, even at the most formal events. Why, the Queen herself has been known to enjoy a waltz on occasion."

"With Prince Albert," Mrs. Lanyon said. "God rest his soul."

Mrs. Sharpe was unmoved. "It may be very well for your lords and ladies, Miss Appersett, but it doesn't change my opinion of it."

No sooner had she finished her sentence than several of the gentlemen entered the drawing room. Among them were Ned and Mr. Murray. They'd been with Sophie's father again, traipsing about the estate for the second day in a row.

Ned leaned down to press a kiss to his mother's cheek. "Your opinion on what?"

"Waltzing," Emily said. "Your mother doesn't approve."

"I won't apologize for my views, Miss Emily," Mrs. Sharpe said. "Humble as they may seem to you."

Mr. Murray winked at Emily. Emily responded by turning a becoming shade of rose.

Sophie frowned. Whatever attraction her sister felt for Walter Murray had only grown since she twisted her ankle. And her feelings didn't appear to be one-sided, either. Each afternoon Mr. Murray whiled away the hours, sitting beside Emily and reading aloud to her from some frivolous text or another.

Sophie didn't know whether she was disgusted or a little envious. Ned had paid her no such attentions since that day in the woods. She supposed it wasn't in his nature to be easy with his affections. At least, not when it came to her. And yet...

And yet he'd said that he admired her. That he wanted her for his own. That she was worth the cost of any improvements to Appersett House.

She glanced up at him. He was still standing near Emily and his mother. He caught her gaze and then—much to her astonishment—gave a subtle jerk of his head in the direction of the doorway. Her brows lifted in question.

"I must go upstairs and change," he told his mother. "I'll be back down for tea."

"You may fetch your father from the billiard room on your way back," Mrs. Sharpe said. "He and the vicar have been in there since breakfast. They'll want some refreshment."

Sophie waited a few moments before laying down her sewing and rising. "If you'll excuse me—"

"Are you going down to the kitchens, Sophie?" Emily interrupted. "Will you tell Cook that I want the iced gingerbread with tea and not that dry loaf she gave us yesterday?"

"Er...yes. I'll tell her." Sophie smoothed a hand over her skirts as she walked to the door. She felt suddenly as if everyone in the room knew what she was about.

She stepped out into the empty hall. There was no sign of Ned anywhere.

Perhaps she'd misinterpreted his gesture? Perhaps he truly had gone up to his room to change?

She lingered a moment, but there seemed no point in waiting. It would only make her conspicuous. She might as well go to the kitchens and see about tea.

With that in mind, she descended the stairs to the first floor. She was nearly at the bottom before she heard him on the steps behind her.

"Sophie." He swiftly caught up with her.

She stopped on the second step, feeling a little foolish when he moved to stand in front of her at the bottom of the stairs. He was still taller than her, but now she need only tilt her head back a fraction for them to see eye to eye.

"Didn't you understand my signal?" he asked.

"I thought I did, but you weren't there, so..."

"You didn't wait very long."

"Really, Ned. What did you expect? I've no experience with subterfuge."

"You seemed to fare all right the night you came to Fleet Street."

Sophie flushed. "That was different."

"Fair enough." He extended a hand to her. "Come. I want to talk with you awhile."

She hesitated before sliding her hand into his. His fingers closed around hers, warm and strong. "Where? Outside? I'm not dressed for it."

"No. Inside. Or, more precisely, in the library. I've been investigating and I've discovered that it's usually empty at this time of day."

Sophie allowed him to lead her across the entry hall and down the corridor to the set of dark, wood-paneled doors that led to the Appersett House library.

The cavernous room, two floors high, was filled to bursting with leather-bound books from generations past. It smelled of beeswax and lemon polish, a fragrance that always reminded Sophie of the long winter days she'd spent as a girl, nestled in one of the oxblood leather chairs by the fire, reading.

"Someone once told me that a well-used private library was the sign of a truly successful gentleman." Ned shut the doors behind him. "A man in possession of one must not only have the ability to read, but the funds to purchase a surfeit of books, and the leisure time to enjoy them."

"I'd never thought of it that way before."

"You wouldn't. You've always had access to this, haven't you?"

"My whole life."

He looked around. "Have you read all of these books?"

She laughed. "Hardly. I can't even claim to have read half of them. They're mostly treatises on agriculture and natural philosophy."

"Not topics very much to your liking, then."

"Not entirely, no. Though I've recently purchased a new book which might qualify as both." She moved to the high wooden shelves on the opposite wall and extracted a volume bound in green cloth. "It's rather controversial," she said as she extended it to him.

Ned took it, his eyes sweeping over the gilt lettering on the spine. "Charles Darwin?"

"Papa doesn't know I purchased it. He wouldn't approve."

"I'm not sure *I* approve." Ned flipped through the pages.

She moved to take it back from him. "Are you the sort of gentleman who'd restrict a lady's reading?"

He held it out of her reach. "Don't be hasty. That isn't what I meant. I simply don't know if I agree with the man's theories."

"And why not? You of all people should see the wisdom in his hypothesis. He believes that living creatures adapt and change in unique and interesting ways. That this very adaptation is what ensures their survival."

"He also believes that human beings derived from monkeys. Or, possibly, worms."

She gave him a look of mild reproof. "You've been reading *Punch*."

"I've seen the caricatures. They're not very flattering to Darwin's theories."

"*Punch* isn't flattering to anyone. I wouldn't put much stock in their opinions. Mr. Darwin's theories on natural selection have been endorsed by countless men of science. And they seem perfectly reasonable to me. What I can understand of them."

He returned her book. His blue eyes grew serious. "Is that really what you think I've done? Adapted and changed to ensure my survival like some plant or animal on an island somewhere?"

"Not exactly. Plants and animals have little in the way of free will. But the idea is the same, isn't it? Adaptation and survival? Only for human beings there's an element of choice involved."

"I've never considered it."

"I have. Indeed, it seems a particularly important point in our modern world. Every day there's a new idea, a new invention. We can no longer be content to stay in the same place, doing the same things as generations before us. We must alter our behavior. We must adapt ourselves to the times or risk being left behind."

Ned looked at her for a long moment. And then, very slowly, an expression of understanding came over his face. But not just understanding, she realized. There was something else there as well. A brief glimmer of compassion. Of tenderness. "You're seeking to rationalize your father's obsession with modernization."

"No! It's not that." She wandered behind one of the leather chairs near the fireplace, her hand resting briefly on the tufted back. "At least, it's not only that."

Ned regarded her from beneath lowered brows as she walked back to the bookcase. "I thought we agreed you were going to leave that particular burden with me."

"It's not so easy to relinquish it. Not when I've been carrying it for as long as I can remember."

"Sophie..." He followed after her, slow and cautious. As if he were stalking one of the wild does in the woods outside Appersett House. "I've been meaning to ask you..."

She turned to re-shelve Mr. Darwin's book. "Yes?"

"The morning we walked together, you said you hadn't wished to marry when you were nineteen, nor when you were twenty, nor one-and-twenty. That it hadn't mattered to you when your father took your dowry." He came to stand behind her. "Why didn't you wish to marry?"

She stilled for an instant, her fingers frozen on the spine of the book. And then she turned back to look at him. "I suspect you already know the answer."

"You're needed here."

"I'm needed here."

Ned's face was grim. "You help to manage things for your family. To keep them from ruin."

"It isn't so heroic as all that. My mother and I haven't that much power. All we can do is make little economies. Carve up the household budget to trim away any fat. Dye our gowns, remake our old hats, that sort of thing. As for the rest...it all comes down to our powers of persuasion. We've been trying to convince Papa to sell his hunters. To retrench. But he's disinclined to make any sacrifices at present."

"He makes no sacrifices at all, that I can see. Nor does your sister."

"We spare her the worst of it. She'd take it too much to heart. It matters so much to her how she looks and what people think of her." Sophie's gaze dropped. She didn't have to look at Ned to know what he was thinking. "You believe she's spoiled."

"Isn't she?"

"A little. But you must understand...Emily is the beauty of the family. The one most likely to marry well—and the one most likely to drain the family coffers if she remains. It only made sense to see her properly outfitted and given a season."

"The family beauty, you say." Ned's voice was deep and warm. "Yet she can't hold a candle to you."

Her heart fluttered. She tried her best to ignore it, even as she raised her eyes back to his. "Yours is the minority view, sir."

Ned rested his hand on the bookshelf at her side. He was so close that her skirts bunched against his legs. "When it comes to you, I'd like to think that, one day, my view will be the only one that matters."

"Second to my own, surely."

His mouth hitched in a fleeting half smile. "You'll not find me a dictator."

It was so absurd, that she smiled, too. "You're making light of it, but I've been independent for a very long while. I'm set in my ways and not likely to change anytime soon."

"You call it independence to live here with your family?"

She lifted her shoulder in a delicate shrug, fully conscious of how his body caged hers against the shelves. It was almost protective the way he loomed over her, his head bent and his arm at her side, surrounding her in the subtle scent of lemon verbena, polished leather, and linen.

One step and she'd be pressed to his chest, her frame engulfed by his much larger one. What might that feel like? Thrilling, she supposed. And dangerous, too. She really didn't know. But the very idea of it made her pulse throb.

"I read what I like and I'm free to come and go as I please," she said. "Within reason."

"Books are important to you."

"Very much. I read whenever I can find a spare moment."

"There haven't been many of those these past days. Since that morning in the woods, I've scarcely seen you outside of the company of the other guests. I'd begun to despair of ever catching you alone."

"You've been no more available than I have. My father commands all your time."

"And my mother, yours."

It was true. She'd been making a special effort to keep his mother entertained. To make her feel at home. Nevertheless...

Sophie sighed. "I don't think she approves of me."

His brows shot up. "Has she said so?"

"Not in so many words."

"In *any* words?"

"She doesn't have to *say* anything. I can tell, when she looks at me, that she finds me lacking." She paused before adding, "Mr. Murray is no great admirer of mine either. After what happened in London, no doubt he thinks me fickle."

"At present, I wonder that Murray thinks anything at all. He seems to have lost his wits over your sister. I can't imagine why."

"I don't suppose you've ever lost your wits over anyone."

He gave her a wry look. "I'm at a baronet's Christmas house party in the wilds of Derbyshire. Frozen solid most nights and obliged to listen to Mrs. Lanyon lament the passing of Prince Albert most days. I think I've lost more than my wits."

Sophie ducked her head to conceal a smile.

"I have another question for you," Ned said.

"Yes?"

"When I kiss you under the mistletoe—and I *am* going to kiss you—would you rather it be in front of your parents and all of creation? Or would you rather it be somewhere private?"

She met his eyes, fully conscious of the heat sweeping up her neck. It was impossible to remain composed under such circumstances. Not when he was looking at her so intently. Not when the butterflies in her stomach were unfurling their wings and soaring into flight.

Good gracious. Was it possible to swoon from the mere mention of kissing?

She moistened her lips. "The mistletoe is only in the drawing room, the doorways, and the main hall. We didn't hang it anywhere else. Certainly nowhere that could be called private."

"That doesn't answer my question."

Her heart skipped a beat. And then another. She tried to ignore it, endeavoring to be sensible about the situation. Businesslike, even. "I'd rather you not kiss me in front of my parents if you can help it. But it's Christmas, so I don't see how—"

"Look what I have."

Sophie watched, breathless, as he reached into the pocket of his waistcoat and withdrew a sprig of mistletoe adorned with three small white berries.

"I'm going to place it just here." He put it on the edge of the shelf above her head. "Unless you object?"

She couldn't seem to summon her voice. When she spoke, the words were the merest whisper. "I don't object."

Ned withdrew his hand from the shelf, but he didn't lower it back to his side. Instead he brought it to her cheek, the back of his fingers tracing a delicate path from her temple to the edge of her jaw. "How soft you are," he murmured. "Even softer than I imagined."

"You've imagined...touching me?"

He gave a dark chuckle. "Often," he said. "Too much for my own good."

She inhaled a tremulous breath. His fingers were warm on her cheek, his touch almost reverent. She'd never dreamed he would handle her with so much care. Not that he'd ever been a brute, but he was so much bigger than her, so tall and strong. She marveled that such a man could be so gentle.

He tipped her chin up on the edge of his hand. Then he bent his head and kissed her very softly on the mouth.

Sophie's eyes fluttered closed as his lips met hers. She'd been kissed beneath the mistletoe before. Childish pecks administered during the Christmases of her youth. But this was no childish peck. Ned's lips were warm and firm, molding perfectly to hers. She listed against him, their mouths clinging together for an endless moment.

And then it was over.

She opened her eyes and blinked up at him, as if waking from a dream that had ended far too soon.

His hand still cupped her chin. He was regarding her intently. "Was that all right?"

She nodded, still incapable of speech. It was more than all right. It was a revelation. Every nerve ending in her body was humming with she knew not what. And all he'd done was caress her face and press a chaste kiss to her lips.

"Do you think you can bear to repeat the experience when next we encounter a sprig of mistletoe?"

Her cheeks burned. A more sophisticated lady might play coy. Might pretend that what had just happened hadn't shaken her to her core. But Ned wasn't blind. And they'd promised to be honest with each other. She saw no reason to prevaricate. "I can more than bear it."

A flash of triumph gleamed in the depths of his blue gaze. "It's hanging in all the doorways, isn't that what you said?"

"And in the drawing room and the main hall. Everywhere in full public view."

He plucked the mistletoe from the shelf above her head and tucked it back into the pocket of his waistcoat. "Then I'd better keep this on hand. Just in case."

ELEVEN

The next day the tree arrived. Some men from the estate drove it up to the front of the house in a long wooden cart. The tall, handsome fir had wide, full branches of deep green. It was so big that part of it dragged on the ground behind the cart, leaving a deep furrow through the snow.

The servants wrestled it into the house and installed it in the main hall where the ceiling was high enough to accommodate its great size. The newly-mended tree skirt was draped round its bottom and then—fortified by cups of tea and glasses of mulled wine—Ned and the other guests were invited to help trim it.

"I expect a woodland creature to crawl out of it," Walter said under his breath. "It's mad to have it in the house."

"Haven't you ever had a Christmas tree, Mr. Murray?" Emily asked. She was established nearby on a straight-backed wooden chair, her injured ankle propped on a tufted footstool. A small wooden crutch leaned at her side. She'd been using it to hobble about.

"Never one of such majestic proportions."

"It has to be big." Sophie walked by carrying a crate of tinsel ornaments. "Anything less would be dwarfed by the size of the hall."

She was wearing an afternoon gown of claret-colored silk with embossed velvet ribbons and fine muslin undersleeves graced with delicate cuffs. The same delectable dress she'd worn to visit Ned in Fleet Street.

He lifted the crate from her arms. "Where would you like it?"

Sophie looked at him and quickly looked away. "Just there, by the tree skirt."

Ned wasn't offended by her response. She'd had just such a reaction at dinner last evening, and then again at breakfast when he sat beside her and their arms had brushed. She was flustered by him. As skittish as a schoolgirl. And he knew why.

It was that kiss.

That brief, all-consuming kiss.

It had been chaste. Respectful. And sweet as anything. All clinging lips and mingled breath. The memory of it had been tormenting him since the moment he'd drawn back from her mouth. He'd spent half the night thinking of it. And the other half dreaming of when he might kiss her again.

"It was Prince Albert who started the tradition," Mrs. Lanyon said. "When he came from Germany to marry the Queen. They always have Christmas trees in Germany."

"We didn't get our first tree until many years after," Ned's father said, twining wire around a tree candle. "Seemed a foolish idea. But it did look fine when it was all decked out."

Lady Appersett smiled as she drifted through the hall. "I think it's a lovely tradition. Don't you agree, Mrs. Sharpe?"

Ned's mother paused in the act of unknotting a ribbon. Her expression was reserved to the point of coldness. "Lovely it is, my lady. And wasteful."

"Wasteful?" Emily echoed.

"Aye. Wasteful, I call it, to cut down a tree merely to dispose of it days later."

"It's tradition," Walter said. "And like all traditions, often more trouble than it's worth. Best to dispense with them all, I say."

"What a humbug you are, Mr. Murray," Emily said. "And to think I cast Mr. Sharpe as Mr. Scrooge and you as Mr. Marley. I daresay it could be the reverse."

Ned exchanged a bewildered glance with Walter.

"What's this about Scrooge and Marley?" Walter asked.

Emily leaned back in her chair, resting her arms on her voluminous green silk skirts. "It's right there on your office door in Fleet Street. Sharpe and Murray. Just like anything out of Mr. Dickens."

Walter cast a pointed look at Emily's crutch. "And who are you in this little pantomime? Tiny Tim?"

"Foolishness," Ned's mother muttered. "Is it any wonder this country is going to rot and ruin with young people talking nothing but nonsense?"

"It's Christmas, mother," Ned said quietly.

She looked at him. "That's no reason to dispense with one's good sense. If one ever had it to begin with."

Sophie, who was tying a red velvet ribbon onto one of the branches, visibly winced at the disapproval in his mother's tone.

Ned's own expression hardened into resolve. This had gone on long enough.

As soon as the opportunity presented itself, he invited his mother to accompany him upstairs on the pretext of selecting more ribbons and tinsel for the tree. He felt a bit guilty at just how readily she obliged him. She clearly wasn't enjoying herself here in Derbyshire. Perhaps it had been a mistake to relay Sophie's invitation to his parents. Perhaps they would have been happier spending the holiday in Cheapside.

"Where are these decorations, then?" she asked.

He opened the door to the drawing room and motioned for her to precede him. "There aren't any."

His mother pursed her lips but didn't question him. She entered the drawing room and took a seat, waiting silently while he shut the doors.

Ned didn't sit down. "Mother, is there anything you wish to tell me? Anything that's happened to put you in such a poor temper?"

She held his gaze, as formidable now in her black silk taffeta and lace matron's cap as she'd been in his youth, when she'd manned the counter in the draper's shop. "You made no mention when she invited us here that Miss Appersett had already rejected you."

Bloody blasted hell. He was going to strangle Walter Murray.

"Do you deny it?" his mother pressed.

He clasped his hands at his back. "It was a misunderstanding. Nothing worth mentioning. We've resolved to try again, as you see."

"She's making a plaything of you, Ned."

A muscle in his jaw twitched. Her words stung. "You don't know her."

"I know her kind. All the young ladies here are just the same. Dazzling you with their airs and graces. And all the while their eyes are fixed firmly on your bank balance."

"I've never been dazzled yet." It wasn't entirely true. And Ned could tell that she knew it.

"She's not good enough for you. None of them are. I was wrong to encourage you to aspire to such a match. You'd be better served with a sensible girl like Marianne Goodbody or Jane Randolph."

Good Lord. Those were two names he hadn't heard in an age. They were well-to-do tradesman's daughters. Girls of his own class who'd been "finished." Whatever that meant. "What is it exactly that you object to in Miss Appersett?" he asked.

"She's inconstant," his mother replied without missing a beat.

"Leaving that aside for the moment."

"How can I? Am I to disregard a facet of her character?"

"I don't ask you to disregard anything, merely to refrain from passing judgment on matters you don't understand."

His mother's mouth tightened. "You think me hard. You always have. But I won't apologize for how I raised you. I brought you up to be strong. To stand fast against whatever comes."

"And every day I thank you for it."

"Aye. You've never been ungrateful. But I know my own son. You've always had a wanting for softness, ever since you were a lad. I won't begrudge you it now. Neither will I see you squander your future on a fine lady who'll treat you no better than a dog once you've wed her."

Ned went still. Her words sank into his flesh like poisonous barbs. "And that's what you believe Miss Appersett will do if I marry her." He searched his mother's face. "Why?"

His mother's expression was as unyielding as her posture. She sat straight and proud, her spine not even touching the back of the silk-upholstered chair. "Her parents are forcing the match. Did you know that?"

"Who said so?"

"Her sister, Miss Emily. Called her the Sacrificial Lamb. Made a joke of it to one of those young ladies from London. How they laughed, the pair of them. I was sitting near the fire. I expect they didn't know I was there. Not that it would have stopped them. These society girls make malicious sport of everything when the gentlemen aren't by."

The Sacrificial Lamb.

Ned inwardly winced. Still, he supposed it could be worse.

He went to his mother and sank down in front of her chair. "Have you ever known me to make poor decisions?"

"Not since you were a lad," she admitted grudgingly.

"Then trust me. I know what I'm about with Miss Appersett."

His mother reached out and briefly touched his cheek. She was not a woman comfortable with displays of affection. She preferred to show her regard through hard work and fierce loyalty. It made the small gesture all the more poignant. "She's going to break your heart, Ned."

He bowed his head for a moment. His mother was right. There was every chance that Miss Appersett would reject him after Christmas. That she'd leave him worse off than he'd been the day she jilted him in Hyde Park. He wasn't afraid to acknowledge it, either to his mother or to himself. "Very likely," he said. "But I'm willing to take the risk."

Sophie studied her cards, doing her level best to ignore Lady Barton's whispered advice on improving her strategy.

It had been Mama's idea that after-dinner card partners be chosen at random from slips of paper placed in a glass bowl. This would prevent the upper-class guests from closing ranks against the lower, she'd said, forcing each table to have a socially diverse group of players.

Sophie had thought it quite a good idea. That is, until she found herself paired with Lady Barton—a compulsive gamester—against the less impressive team of Mr. Fortescue and Miss Tunstall.

Ned was faring no better. He was partnered with Mrs. Lanyon against a stammering London debutante and an elderly squire with an ear trumpet. They were seated at a nearby card table in the drawing room, close enough that Sophie could hear every word Mrs. Lanyon uttered about the untimely death of Prince Albert.

She stole a swift glance at Ned over the top of her cards.

Tomorrow night was the Christmas ball. It was expected to be a crush. Invitations had gone out to friends and relations in both London and Derbyshire. Even people who'd shunned the house party were expected to make an appearance at the ball. There would be an orchestra. There would be waltzing.

More to the point, there would be waltzing with Ned.

It made her slightly giddy to think of it.

There'd been no more romantic encounters with him since that kiss in the library, but she'd daily been in his company. She'd seen how respectful he was of his parents and how kind and solicitous he'd been to her mother and even, on occasion, to her sister.

She'd observed his unfailing patience when dealing with those who others dismissed as tedious, long-winded bores.

He was a good listener. Not given much to words, but always attentive in his silence.

A quality that was on full display.

"He and the Queen married for love," Mrs. Lanyon said. "How his death must be affecting her! She will be grieving for a long while, I expect. Longer than is the custom. A lady does not recover from such a loss in a few years' time."

"Nor would a gentleman," Ned murmured.

"You think not, Mr. Sharpe? In my experience, gentlemen don't feel the loss of a much-loved spouse as deeply as we ladies do. I've seen it time and again when my brother counsels newly bereaved widowers. They're saddened, to be sure, but I can detect no permanent injury to their hearts and minds. Do you find differently, sir?"

"I cannot speak for all gentlemen," Ned said as he played a card. "But if I loved and lost, I believe I would feel it rather keenly."

Sophie's heart turned over.

"Miss Appersett," Lady Barton said sharply. "It's *your* turn."

"Yes, of course. I do beg your pardon." She played a card of her own. The wrong card, if Lady Barton's expression was any judge. But Sophie didn't care. Her thoughts were far from the game.

She remembered what Ned had said on his first day at Appersett House when she asked if he considered himself a warm person. It had been the truth. He didn't often show emotion, but he felt things deeply. She recognized that now.

And that wasn't the only thing she recognized.

He was a good man. So much more than his stern appearance. She wanted…

Oh, but she didn't know what she wanted. She couldn't put it into words. Couldn't even organize it into a coherent thought.

If only she'd met him under different circumstances. If only Papa didn't keep stealing him away to show him things on the estate or to huddle with him in his study. She'd tried to put it out of her head, to let Ned shoulder the burden of it, but the weight of Papa's mania for improvements weighed on her. Even more now that she realized how much she liked Ned. It hadn't mattered as much before if Papa scared him away. But now…

She couldn't imagine what she'd do if Ned decided she wasn't worth it. If, after Christmas, he simply packed up his things and returned to London.

Her worries were only intensified the following morning when Ned and Mr. Murray once again accompanied Papa out onto the estate. Sophie didn't know what they were doing. Looking at the gas works again, perhaps.

The rest of the guests were occupied with final preparations for the ball. Her mother and Emily had things well in hand. For once, Sophie wasn't needed. She slipped out at the first opportunity, making her way down the stairs and across the hall to the library. She wanted some privacy. A chance to curl up with a book and catch her breath.

Instead, as she passed the door to Papa's study, she found herself hesitating. Before she could think twice, she turned the doorknob and let herself inside.

The study was Papa's private domain. It was where he met with his steward. Where he wrote letters and balanced the accounts. Sophie had seen the ledgers once. They'd been filled with red ink and scribbled notations. She didn't think she'd ever shut a book so quickly. The contents had horrified her.

There were no ledgers on his desk now. She crept up to the tall burled walnut monstrosity and scanned the surface. It was riddled with crystal paperweights, inkwells, and haphazard stacks of what looked to be tradesman's bills. Her fingers itched to go through them, but she restrained herself.

Across the floor of the study was a standing globe in a heavy frame, a line of short bookcases with glass doors locked tight, and an inlaid drum table on which a map was draped. No. Not a map. Something finer. A drawing or a sketch of some kind.

Curious, she moved closer, her eyes drifting over the fine lines and angles.

It was Appersett House. A detailed plan of the layout, complete with cross-sections of the interior of the walls and the spaces beneath the floorboards.

"Sophia!" Papa bellowed from the doorway. "What are you doing in here?"

Sophie turned around with a start.

Her father closed the distance between them in a few hurried strides and snatched the plans from the table. "Why aren't you with the others?"

"They don't require me at the moment. I was going to the library to read awhile." She followed her father as he folded up the plans and went to his desk. He sat heavily in the chair behind it. "Are those plans for the new plumbing?"

He scowled. "What do you know of that?"

"Only what you've said on occasion. And…what Mr. Sharpe has told me."

"Sharpe's been telling tales about my project, has he?" Papa looked outraged. "Can't say I'm surprised. He's got no vision. No appreciation for progress. Murray, on the other hand…"

Sophie's eyes narrowed. "What about Mr. Murray?"

"He's the son of a stonemason. As wealthy as Sharpe in his own right, but with an appreciation for building and renovation." Her father scrubbed at his face. He looked tired and irritable. Not the best time to approach him with her problems. Even so…

"Papa, you don't really think having plumbing installed is a good idea, do you?"

"Why wouldn't I?"

She rested her fingers lightly on the edge of his desk, casting about for a diplomatic way to phrase things. There wasn't one. "Because we can't afford it. Surely you must see—"

"Of course we can afford it! Why do you think I permitted Sharpe to court you? He's got more than enough to cover the plumbing, and all the rest of it besides."

Her breath stopped. For several seconds, she could do nothing but stare at her father. "The rest of it? What rest of it?"

Papa had the grace to redden. "Trifles," he said with a dismissive wave of his hand. "Paint. Roof tiles. Gravelling the drive. Nothing that will bankrupt the fellow."

She pressed a hand to her midriff. Her corset felt suddenly as if it had been laced two inches too tight. "We don't need it."

"I'll be the judge of that."

"We don't need it," she said again.

Something in her voice made her father sit up straight at his desk. Any hint of embarrassment about his plans evaporated. "Don't take that tone with me, young miss."

In the past, Sophie might have quailed at the hint of iron in his words. But today, try as she might to respect him, there was no backing down. "You won't be content until you ruin us. Until you ruin him."

"I'm in no mood for dramatics," Papa snapped.

Sophie didn't care what he was in the mood for. "You'll make him despise me, do you realize that? Any hope there might be for my happiness...you'll destroy it with your constant demands on him."

"I have a responsibility to the estate."

"You have a responsibility to us! To Mama, Emily, and me. How can you not see that?"

Papa gritted his teeth. "I have no heir," he ground out.

"You have me. And you have Emily. And—"

"Two daughters. What use are you to me? You'll marry and take your husband's name. You aren't my heirs. This house will be my only legacy. The only thing of value left when I'm gone. The only thing that will endure. I have a duty to see it right."

"Oh, Papa." She shook her head. "I love Appersett House, too, but it's not flesh and blood. Emily and I are what's real. Mama is what's real. This house is—"

"It's my legacy. And if you think I care two snaps of my finger whether that makes a draper's son despise the lot of us—"

"That draper's son is the gentleman you mean me to marry."

His expression turned mulish. No different from Emily's when she was in a temper. "It's the only way. Even with your sister's dowry—"

Sophie barely managed to suppress a gasp. "What about Emily's dowry?"

Papa dropped his gaze. "Things have arisen. Necessities for the estate. I owe you no explanation."

"Is it...is it gone? Did you spend it all?"

"I told you. It doesn't concern you. Now be off with you, Sophie. I have work to do."

A heavy blanket of gloom settled over her, snuffing out the last spark of her holiday cheer. "Does Mama know?" she asked softly.

Her father hung his head.

She needed no other answer. She let herself out of his study, shutting the door firmly behind her.

TWELVE

Emily sat at her dressing table, head bowed as Sophie brushed her hair. Their eyes met in the mirror. "I don't know why you prefer my limited skills to Annie's," Sophie said.

"She doesn't do it as well as you."

Sophie doubted that very much. Annie had been with them several years and had grown adept at managing their thick tresses. Granted, she was no French lady's maid with a talent for dazzling coiffures, but she could handle a brush and hairpins well enough. "She's going to arrange my hair for the ball."

"How will you wear it?" Emily asked.

Sophie parted her sister's hair into two sections. "A bandeau bouffant, probably. Or perhaps a crown of plaits."

"The same as always."

"It's easiest. And if it comes unpinned during the dancing, I can repair it myself."

"Why must you always be so practical?"

"One of us must be."

"Well, it shan't be me," Emily declared. "My hair will be woven with a waterfall of flowers. Just like the picture we saw in Mama's magazine."

Sophie nodded. After her father's revelation, she was determined to indulge her sister. There would be time enough for Emily to learn the truth about her dowry after Christmas. Until then, they could all try and enjoy themselves. "Rolls at each side and three rolls at the back, wasn't it? It's going to take a great deal of pins, Emmy. You'll have a dreadful headache by the time the night is over."

"I don't care. As long as it looks as it should. And as long as no one else will arrive with the same coiffure."

Sophie reached for one of the rats on her sister's dressing table. Made of hair collected from Emily's brush each evening, the homemade hairpiece would be used to pad out the rolls and help them keep their shape. "Is there anyone particular you wish to impress?"

Emily pursed her lips. "Possibly."

"You know you can talk to me."

"Not about matters of the heart, I can't. You wouldn't understand."

"You're very harsh." Sophie finished rolling a section of Emily hair around the rat. She sank in a pin to secure it. "Do you think you're the only young lady who's ever developed a tendre for an unsuitable gentleman?"

"How is Mr. Murray unsuitable? He's as wealthy as Mr. Sharpe. Indeed, he partners with him in all his investments. Besides, I actually *like* Mr. Murray. He's not carved from a slab of granite. He's funny and thoughtful and...he makes me laugh."

Sophie concentrated on rolling the next section. "That's all very well, dear, but I thought you wanted to marry a title?"

"Yes, but I didn't know...I didn't expect..." Emily exhaled a frustrated breath. "I don't want to make a mistake."

"How could you?"

"By doing what I'm told. Or not doing what I'm told. By choosing the wrong gentleman. You can't comprehend what it's like to struggle over such decisions, Sophie. You're too perfect."

"Perfect?" Sophie caught her sister's gaze in the mirror. "I'm the furthest thing from perfect, Emmy. I have to struggle every day with doing the right thing."

"At least you know what the right thing is."

"Sometimes I don't. Some days I'm filled with doubt." She ran the brush through a fresh section of her sister's hair. "And some days I know what the right thing is and I don't want to do it. I'd rather be selfish and think only of myself."

"But in the end, you always do what's expected of you."

"Expected by whom? Mama and Papa? Not always."

"You do when it matters," Emily said. "You're even willing to accept the gentleman they chose for you, though I know you don't like him."

"You're wrong. I do like Mr. Sharpe. And Mama and Papa didn't choose him for me. He chose me for himself. They merely encouraged the match."

"That's a nice way of putting it, but I know how it truly is. And you're not to think I don't care, just because I bicker with you and lose my temper at all your economies. I would save you from marrying him if I could."

Sophie's lips curved into a smile. She was both touched and a little amused by her sister's concern. "There's no need to save me, Em. Mr. Sharpe hasn't even proposed yet. He may never."

"Good. It will spare you the scandal of breaking a betrothal."

Sophie laughed as she anchored the last pin in Emily's hair, securing the final cluster of flowers. "There. What do you think?"

Emily preened. "Oh yes, this is just what I had in mind. And the pins only hurt a little."

"I'm glad. Now bend your head and I'll give it a good spray." Sophie fetched the glass atomizer of liquid bandoline. It was made of a clear gum solution, the stickiness of which would keep Emily's hair in place throughout the ball.

With her sister's hair done, Sophie could at last retire to her room to attend to her own toilette. Annie quickly arranged her hair and helped her dress.

Sophie's gown for the Christmas ball was really a combination of two outdated evening dresses the village seamstress had made over to match a plate in the *Englishwoman's Domestic Magazine*. The resulting ball gown was a fashionable—and quite daring—creation of wine-colored crêpe over wine-colored silk, with double skirts, tiny fluttering sleeves, and a V-shaped neckline cut low in both front and back.

The whole of it was adorned with sprays of gold flowers, oaken leaves, and gilded acorns. Annie stuck some into Sophie's hair for good measure.

"You look ever so handsome, miss," she said, beaming.

Sophie paused a moment to admire herself in the pier glass. "It came out well, didn't it? It looks almost new."

"No one could tell who didn't know."

Satisfied, Sophie pulled on her gloves, gathered up her little paper fan that doubled as a dance card, and made her way down the hall.

Evening had fallen and the corridors were lit with the soft glow of gaslight, an ever-present reminder of her father's extravagance. For what must be the hundredth time, she resolved not to think about it. Fretting over their finances would serve no purpose except ruining the ball for her. And why should she do that? The money had already been spent. The guests were here. The food was ordered. And the orchestra was setting up in the ballroom.

There would be ample time to weep over their situation after Christmas.

For now, she would plaster a smile on her face and greet the guests with the rest of her family.

She'd gone no more than a few feet when she saw Ned coming from the opposite direction.

Her heart performed its now familiar somersault.

He was garbed in black and white evening dress, his dark hair combed into meticulous order and his short side-whiskers trimmed close along the hard line of his jaw. He looked elegant and commanding. So much like the severe gentleman who'd courted her in London that she almost forgot how dear he'd become to her.

And then he smiled.

Good heavens.

A flush of pleasure suffused her chest, as warm and glowing as the gaslight that surrounded her. She met him halfway down the hall.

His blue gaze drifted over her. "Sophie."

"Hello."

She'd never been more aware of him. Of the way he looked, so tall and handsome. Of the sound of his voice, so much deeper and huskier than usual. Her bosom rose and fell on a self-conscious breath. His gaze dropped and lingered there for a fraction of second. She was sure she blushed. She could feel the heat of it seeping over the wide expanse of exposed flesh at her neck and shoulders.

"Sophie," he said again. His Adam's apple bobbed on a swallow. "You look..." But he only shook his head, seemingly lost for words.

"You've seen me in evening dress before," she reminded him, her cheeks burning. "A ball gown isn't so very different."

"Isn't it? It feels a world of difference to me."

"You approve, I take it."

"I more than approve. I stand in awe."

Well.

"Is that your dance card?" He touched a white-gloved finger to the dangling fan at her wrist.

"It is."

"And how many dances may I claim?"

"How many would you like?"

Ned's voice deepened. "All of them."

Sophie's lips tilted in a bemused smile. "You don't even know if I'll make a good partner."

"I know." He spoke with unerring confidence. "Shall I put my name down for all of your waltzes?"

"There are four waltzes this evening. And I can dance no more than three dances with any one gentleman."

"Three, then."

She nodded and Ned made short work of penciling his name into her dance card. When he'd finished, he looked at her again, the weight of his gaze making her feel a tiny bit flustered. "What is it?"

"You," he said simply. And then: "I've never seen anyone look so vivid under the gaslight."

"Oh, that." Sophie gave her skirts a little rustle over her crinoline. "Most colors lose their brilliancy by gaslight. But this particular shade is complemented by it. The gaslight deepens the hue. Makes it warmer and richer, like a full-bodied red wine. Or so my seamstress claims."

"She's not wrong. It looks... *You* look..." He made a noise low in his throat. "I'm not sure I can let you—"

"What?"

But he didn't seem disposed to answer. Instead, he caught her hand and pulled her into a small alcove off the hall. Once upon a time, it had contained a marble pedestal holding an expensive sculpture. Now, the alcove was empty—and just large enough to fit the both of them standing face to face.

Ned bent his head. "I don't know if I can let you dance with anyone else. Not without kissing you first."

Oh my.

Sophie's heart skipped several beats. A wall sconce outside the alcove flickered, casting a half shadow over Ned's face. This was to be her gaslight kiss, then. Just as he'd promised her. "We can't. Anyone might see."

He brought his hand to cradle her face. "We're quite hidden."

She refrained from pointing out that her skirts were spilling out into the hall. At this stage it didn't seem to matter. He wanted to kiss her. And she very much wanted to kiss him back. She raised her hand to curl about his neck, the movement unsteady and uncertain. "I'm afraid I'll crush your cravat," she admitted, a little sheepishly.

Ned's expression softened with something like tenderness. "Never mind my cravat."

And then his mouth covered hers.

Sophie's eyes fell shut and her breath stuttered. For a moment, she stood still as a statue, just as she had the first time. But it was impossible to remain so. Not with her hand curved tight around his neck. Not with his arms moving to encircle her waist, drawing her flush against his chest.

Her lips softened beneath his, half-parting under the gentle, searching pressure of his mouth. She felt the warmth of his breath. The clutch of his fingers at her corseted waist. And they kissed each other. There was no other way to describe it. They kissed *each other.* Like equals. Like partners. Both active participants in what had to be the most intimate experience of Sophie's entire life.

"My God," he breathed when they finally broke apart. It sounded like a groan. Or possibly a prayer. "My God, Sophie."

She held his gaze, lips still half-parted as she tried to catch her breath. "Was that all right?"

Ned ran a hand over his face. And then he gave her a lop-sided smile. It was the smile of a much younger man. Smitten and foolish. A little rueful. It was utterly unlike any smile he'd ever given her before.

Sophie's heart clutched. Had she finally managed to put the stern and forbidding Mr. Edward Sharpe out of countenance? To render him no more than a speechless schoolboy?

Or perhaps not so speechless.

"It was more than all right," he said. "It was perfect. You're perfect."

It was the worst possible thing he could have said. Especially following Emily's accusations of perfection.

Not that it ruined the moment. She didn't think anything could. Still...

She'd rather he thought of her as a woman than some glorified feminine ideal

"I'm not perfect." She backed away from him, or at least as far as the alcove would allow. "But I am obliged to you for the kiss."

"And I to you."

"Well, then."

His lop-sided smile widened. "Well, then."

The sound of musicians tuning their instruments drifted up the stairs. The ball was about to commence. "I shouldn't linger. The guests will be arriving soon. My parents will expect me in the hall to welcome them." She paused. "Will you escort me downstairs?"

"Er...you go ahead. I'll stay here awhile."

"You're right. We'd do better to go down separately. We wouldn't wish to be remarked."

"No, indeed." He caught at her hand as she moved to leave. "Sophie?"

She met his eyes. "Yes?"

He looked steadily back at her. "I mean to claim those waltzes."

"They're yours, Ned," she said. But what she really meant was *I'm yours*. And, as she slipped out of the alcove and hurried down the hall, she suspected he knew it.

THIRTEEN

The ballroom at Appersett House was magnificent. It was also hot, stuffy, and overcrowded. The crystal gasoliers and the gas jets in the gilded wall sconces worked in concert with the guests to suck the oxygen from the room. Three ladies had already fainted. It was quite an achievement—and not at all a negative one. Indeed, no party was counted a success unless it was an absolute crush.

As the orchestra played the last notes of Ned's final waltz with Sophie, he contemplated inviting her for a walk on the terrace. The snow would be a refreshing change from the cloying scent of men's pomade, women's perfume, and human perspiration. Besides, he wanted to kiss her again and the odds of finding any privacy indoors were next to nil.

She stepped back as their dance ended, returning his short bow with a shallow curtsy. "I told you I wouldn't be a good partner. I must have trod on your toes three times."

"Four times. Not that I'm keeping count."

She gave him a laughing grimace. "How mortifying. I'm not usually so clumsy."

"You're tired, that's all. The gentlemen have danced you off your feet." Ned didn't think she'd ever lacked a partner. She was a firm favorite with both the gentry and villagers alike.

"You've been no less popular."

"I've been *much* less popular."

"Nonsense. You danced with Mrs. Lanyon and Miss Tunstall and I don't know how many others."

A smile played at the corners of his mouth. "Were you keeping count?"

"You needn't look so smug. I only noticed because Mrs. Lanyon fainted after the lancers." Sophie cast a quick look around. "I hope she's feeling better now. I don't see her anywhere."

"My mother took her upstairs to rest in one of the guest rooms."

"Bless your mother. She's not having very much fun, is she?"

"She dislikes frivolity. And I'm sure the lack of fresh air doesn't help. She'd rather have a few moments of quiet than linger at the side of a ballroom. Even if those moments are occupied wafting smelling salts under someone's nose."

Sophie sighed as Ned led her from the floor. "I can't say I blame her. It's so dreadfully close in here."

He didn't disagree. "Would you care for some punch? Or—if you have a wrap—perhaps you might accompany me out onto the terrace?"

"Both, if you please."

"Which would you like first?"

"Punch. I'll come with you to the refreshment table. We can..." Sophie's voice trailed off, her attention arrested by something happening across the ballroom.

Ned followed her gaze. Sir William and Lady Appersett stood at the edge of the polished wood floor, engaged in a heated conversation with Emily...and Walter Murray.

"What in heaven...?" Sophie wondered under her breath.

Ned's stomach clenched in a knot. He had a sinking feeling. A feeling which was only intensified by the sight of Walter's hand on Emily Appersett's back. Ned watched it move in a soothing, and wholly proprietary, circle. As if Walter was trying to calm the agitated young lady. As if...

Damn it all to hell.

Hadn't he warned the man? Hadn't he told him...?

"Something's happened. They're leaving." Sophie moved to follow after them.

Ned caught at her hand. "Wait. I'll go with you."

She looked at him, her eyes filled with helpless dread. "Ned..."

"I know. It will be all right." He squeezed her hand before tucking it through his arm. "There's nothing broken that can't be mended."

Sophie didn't respond. Not in words. But her fingers clenched his sleeve as he escorted her from the ballroom.

Sir William and Lady Appersett convened with Walter and their younger daughter in the library. Lady Appersett was settling herself in a chair when Ned entered with Sophie on his arm.

Sophie instantly let go of him and went to her sister. "Emily...?"

The two of them exchanged hushed words while Walter lingered nearby. Ned caught his friend's gaze and held it, unflinching. Walter turned a dull red. Ned was amazed that he still could. The man was clearly shameless.

"This is a fine kettle of fish." Sir William paced in front of the fireplace. "At the ball of all places. Where anyone might overhear."

"Keep a level head, my dear," Lady Appersett murmured to him. "We must *all* try to keep a level head."

Emily scoffed. "It's only a proposal, Mama. It isn't as if I've been compromised."

"Only a proposal!" Sir William turned on Walter, pointing at him with a shaking finger. "You, sir, are a deceiving blackguard. To come into my home under false pretenses. To approach my daughter—"

"My proposal of marriage was made in earnest," Walter said. "I mean your daughter no disrespect."

"It's not the proposal I object to, man. It's the way you went about it. Have you no sense of the manner in which these things are done? You should have come to me first. There are contracts to hammer out. Settlements and the like."

"Mr. Murray doesn't view me in those terms, Papa." Emily moved closer to her still-blushing beau. "I'm not a boring old business arrangement."

Ned stole a glance at Sophie. Her expression was shuttered, her arms folded tightly at her waist.

Is that what *she* thought? That she was a business arrangement to him? Nothing more than a dry negotiation of contracts and settlements? Granted, when he'd wished to court her, he'd gone to her father first. He'd done everything exactly as the *Gentleman's Book of Etiquette* advised. Pursuing Sophia Appersett had been the most important decision of his life. He hadn't wanted to put a foot out of line.

Only now did he realize that, in his zeal to do everything right, he might have inadvertently done everything wrong.

He'd wanted so badly to win her. To show himself a gentleman equal to those of her rank and breeding. As a result, there had been no romance in his pursuit. No impetuousness.

Unlike Walter Murray's pursuit of her sister. An unsanctioned courtship filled with teasing and flirting and God knows what else.

"I wouldn't like it if he'd asked you first," Emily went on. "As if he didn't care for me at all and only cared for my dowry."

Walter glanced down at her with an expression of affectionate indulgence. "Your father's right. I should have asked him for your hand before I approached you." He looked at Sir William and Lady Appersett in turn. "I apologize for my impulsiveness, but I love your daughter. And I believe she loves me as well."

Emily beamed. "Mr. Murray is going to take me on an Italian holiday for our honeymoon."

Sophie's face was white. "Emmy, that's all very well, but..."

"I know you think I want a title, Sophie. I thought so too. But I'd far rather marry for love. One of us may as well. And you must agree—"

"That isn't it," Sophie said. "That isn't it at all. Tell her, Papa."

Sir William paled. "Sophia...this is neither the time, nor the place—"

"Your father has spent your dowry, my love," Lady Appersett said. "There is naught but one hundred pounds left of it."

What the devil?

Ned was sure his jaw dropped. He took in the expressions of everyone in the room in one swift, comprehensive glance. Sophie and her father were bloodless and still. Lady Appersett appeared resigned. Emily's face was reddening with something like outrage. And Walter...

Walter had the temerity to laugh, blast him.

"I can't say I'm surprised," he said. "Not that it matters one jot. I'd take Emily in her underclothes, even without your blessing."

Lady Appersett's lips twitched. "Mr. Murray," she chastised with a small shake of her head. "The things you say."

Walter grinned. "Naturally, I'd rather have your blessing. If you'll give it to us."

Sir William nodded very slowly. "There are benefits to having a mason's son in the family. I can see that now. You understand the estate better than some." He flashed a narrow look at Ned. "But this is all highly irregular. There are settlements to consider and—"

"And I will be at your disposal tomorrow for however long it takes to sort them," Walter said. "As I've told your daughter, you'll not find me tight-fisted."

Some of the color returned to Sir William's face. "Then this is a cause for celebration. My dear? Call for some champagne."

Lady Appersett stood and went to the bell pull that hung beside the fireplace. A footman responded to the summons almost instantly and, after a few words with Lady Appersett, left just as swiftly.

"Shall we make an announcement?" Walter asked.

"As to that..." Sir William tugged at his cravat. "Let's not be too hasty. We'll keep the news in the family for now. I'll determine the best way to announce it at a more appropriate time."

Ned exchanged a brief look with Walter. They both knew full well that a baronet's daughter wedding a tradesman was no cause for public rejoicing. Once married, Emily would be ostracized from the society to which she'd been born. There would be no more invitations to fashionable soirees, nor hobnobbing with earls and viscounts. She'd be the wife of a wealthy man, true. But hers would be a very different sort of life than the one she'd had thus far.

"I can't believe you spent my dowry," Emily said to her father. "You promised you wouldn't touch it."

Sir William waved her away. "Your betrothed will understand when he sees the improvements I've made. And I have greater plans still. It will make the gaslight pale in comparison."

"The gas works can explode for all I care," Emily retorted. "And you—" She turned on her sister. "How long have you known?"

"Not long," Sophie said. "Papa told me only yesterday."

"Why didn't you tell me?"

"I would have done after Christmas. There was no point in ruining your holiday. There was still the ball to get through."

"You sound just like Mama."

Sophie gave her sister a faint smile. "I shall take that as a compliment."

Walter crossed the library to join Ned as the sisters talked. His advance was cautious to the point of exaggeration. "You'd like to punch me in the face, wouldn't you?"

"I'd like to disembowel you with a teaspoon."

Walter winced. "Ouch."

"Didn't I warn you?"

"Have a heart, Ned. Some things can't be avoided. You'd know what I mean if you'd ever been in love. It's not something you can tally on a ledger."

Ned's expression tightened. Walter didn't know a blasted thing. It was true, the morning she'd jilted him, Ned had said he didn't love Sophia Appersett. He'd only admired her. Only thought her a beautiful creature. But things had changed. His feelings for her were…

Good God, he didn't know what he was feeling. But it wasn't some giddy insensible emotion. It was deeper than that, and far finer. Something that warmed his blood and made his chest tighten whenever he saw her. Something that made him want to kiss her as he had in the alcove. To hold her safe in his arms for hours, inhaling the soft fragrance of her rose-scented hair.

More than that, it was a compulsion—an all-consuming desire—to make the way smooth for her. To alleviate her burdens and see her safe and well.

Perhaps he was being too pragmatic, too reasonable. After all, romantic love didn't work in terms of plans and logic. It made one reckless and foolish. Willing to take risks and damn the consequences. By that measure, perhaps Walter was right. Perhaps he wasn't in love with Sophia Appersett.

But by heaven, he loved her.

The realization nearly knocked him over.

"I've fancied her since we first met," Walter admitted, oblivious to Ned's epiphany. He looked across the room at his intended. "The little termagant. She's led me a merry dance."

Sophie and Emily were standing beside the very row of bookcases where Ned had first kissed Sophie.

"Are you happy for me?" Emily asked.

"Are *you* happy, Emmy?"

"Terribly happy."

"Then I'm glad of it." Sophie embraced her sister.

Emily smiled. Her voice sank to a poor apology for a whisper. "Didn't I tell you I'd save you if I could?"

Ned's gaze jerked to Sophie's. His heart thumped hard.

"You're free now, Sophie," Emily said. "You needn't sacrifice yourself to save the family. I've saved it all on my own."

"Oh Emily, I—"

"You don't have to thank me. I'll consider it thanks enough when you resume your life as it was before. You were happy then. Happy and free. And now, you shall be so again."

Very slowly Walter turned to face Ned, his mouth open as if poised to offer his apologies—or his condolences.

"Don't," Ned warned.

But Walter couldn't be silenced. "Damnation, Ned. I didn't think."

Ned could summon no words in reply. He was too stunned. Too utterly dumbfounded. Because he hadn't thought either. He'd never once considered.

With Walter Murray offering his wealth to save the Appersett family, what need would anyone have of Edward Sharpe?

FOURTEEN

Christmas Eve dawned bright and clear, the sun shining weakly over the snow-covered Derbyshire landscape. The windows were frosted with ice, the fires going full force in the grates. The servants had been running up and down the stairs since dawn, hauling wood and coals and hot water for the guests.

Sophie spent most of the day overseeing activities with the younger ladies and gentlemen. They wrapped last-minute gifts, built snowmen, and some of the more daring had gone sledding. Later, they played a game of charades while drying out in front of the drawing room fire.

Meanwhile, Papa had taken the rest of the gentlemen hunting. Did Ned shoot? Did Mr. Murray? Sophie hadn't the slightest idea. All she knew was that it was a dratted nuisance. What was Papa thinking, spiriting Ned away when she most wished to speak with him?

She'd seen the way he looked at her last night in the library. He'd become cold and remote before her eyes, clasping his hands at his back and standing apart from them all.

He'd overheard Emily, of course. All her little gibes about Sophie being free and not having to make a sacrifice. It was so much silliness, but Ned wouldn't know that. He had no reason to doubt Emily's assertions.

When at last he returned to the house, he kept his distance from her. He was never rude. Indeed, he was unfailing civil—just as he'd been in London. He was also stern and reserved and so infuriatingly reluctant to utter five words together that Sophie felt as if they'd fallen right back to where they'd started.

It intimidated her a little, just as it had done during the early months of their courtship. And yet, she now understood that beneath that icy exterior, Ned was probably simmering with hurt.

She wished she was bold enough to simply grab his hand and pull him into an alcove as he'd done to her the day before. But she didn't want a stolen moment with him. She needed more time. More privacy. And she knew just how to get it.

Her mother had organized sleigh rides for the evening and, for once during the course of this accursed house party, things went according to plan.

The sleighs arrived in front of Appersett House in the early evening, just as the sun was beginning to set. The horses had bells on their bridles and the sleighs themselves were draped in red velvet bows and greenery.

It had stopped snowing for the moment and, as the sky darkened, the stars slowly made themselves visible.

Sophie was bundled up in her cloak and fur muff, her hair twisted up into an invisible hair net trimmed in velvet. Emily and Mr. Murray had already climbed into one of the sleighs and trotted off, leaving her waiting at the bottom of the steps. She saw Ned standing at the doors to the house, listening to something his mother was saying. His head was bent, his face somber.

Mrs. Sharpe looked equally grim. And when, a moment later, she and Ned turned and looked at her, Mrs. Sharpe's lined face seemed to grow grimmer still.

Sophie raised a gloved hand to them. When coupled with her weak smile, she was sure she looked as if she was going to be ill. She certainly felt that way. A sickening sense of foreboding roiled heavily in her stomach. It was nerves, she told herself. The knowledge did little to calm her as Ned descended the stairs.

"Are you waiting for me?" he asked. Like her, he was bundled up against the cold, his black wool overcoat buttoned up over the suit he'd worn to dinner. She could just make out the top of his cravat as it brushed the line of his jaw.

"I assumed we would go together," she said. "Unless...I suppose I could wait for one of the other gentlemen to take me. The sleighs only seat two, or else I would have already gone with the vicar and Mrs. Lanyon. They left right before Mr. Murray and my sister."

"You shouldn't be standing out here in the snow. You'll catch your death."

"I didn't want to miss you again. I was hoping we might have a chance to talk."

He gave her a look that was hard to read. And then he nodded. "Yes. I expected as much."

She slid both her hands into her muff. "We can find somewhere inside, if you like."

"If you'd prefer."

"I thought a sleigh ride might give us more privacy."

"Of course."

The feeling of foreboding in Sophie's stomach intensified. Ned's face was so peculiarly blank. She wished she could tell what he was thinking. "Can you handle the ribbons?"

For the first time, a glint of some emotion flickered in his eyes. It may have been wry humor. "I'm not completely incompetent in the country."

"No?" She endeavored to keep her voice light. "Did you shoot anything this morning?"

He extended his hand to help her up into the sleigh. "Does a tree branch count?"

She smiled, settling her skirts around her as Ned climbed into the sleigh at her side. "So little experience and already as skillful as my father."

Ned draped a carriage blanket over her lap with a low chuckle. "He isn't very good at it, is he?"

"I believe he likes the tramping around out of doors part better than the actual shooting. He's never been particularly adept. Indeed, at one point, I'd considered that we might allow hunting parties from London to make use of our woods next season. For a fee, of course."

"Very entrepreneurial." Ned took the ribbons from the groom. "And, thanks to Murray, completely unnecessary."

The sleigh started off with a jingle of bells as the horses surged into motion. Sophie could see no one else about. The other sleighs had gone in different directions and at varying speeds. For all intents and purposes, she and Ned were alone.

She cast him a sidelong glance. His profile was hard, his blue gaze fixed on the snowy expanse ahead of them. "Did you know he was going to propose to my sister?"

"I hadn't a clue."

"You were with them today, weren't you? In my father's study?"

"They wanted my input on the settlements." He returned her glance. "Murray's been excessively generous. You won't ever have to worry again."

She stared out at the snow. Ned was right. The burden of her family's finances was finally gone. Papa's profligacy could now be Mr. Murray's problem. He seemed keen enough to subsidize new plumbing, re-graveled drives, and the like. Perhaps being a stonemason's son really did give him an appreciation for repairs and renovations.

"I confess it is a relief," she said. "I hadn't realized how much until I woke up this morning. It was as if a weight had been lifted from my shoulders."

"No doubt."

"Emily is proud of herself for managing it. She believes she saved me from making a martyr of myself."

"And how do you feel?" he asked with a casualness that, on any other occasion, might have made her think he didn't care in the least.

"I'm still trying to accustom myself to the new reality."

"Which is?"

"That my life is my own again. That I need no longer do anything purely out of duty. From now on, any decisions I make about my future will be mine alone." She felt him look at her, but she didn't return his gaze. She continued to stare straight ahead, hands clasped tight within her muff as she gathered her courage. "Would you like to marry me?"

Ned's expression hardened. "You already know what my intentions were. I made them clear enough to your father when I asked leave to court you in London."

"You misunderstand me. I'm not inquiring about what your intentions were then. I'm asking you if you'll marry me now."

He jerked his head to stare at her.

She hesitated. "Well, not precisely now. In a few months. Or a few weeks. Whenever is convenient."

His lips half parted as realization registered slowly on his face. That same jaw that had tensed seconds before went slack and his throat bobbed on a swallow. He was stunned. Staggered. Or—very possibly—horrified.

But Sophie was driven to continue, her words tumbling out in an impassioned rush. "I think I fell a little bit in love with you the night I came to your office in Fleet Street. And I've grown to love you more each day. So, if you have any feelings for me at all—if you have any inclination—I'd like very much for you to marry me and take me back to London. Because I do love you, Ned. And though I have no dowry, I would try very hard to be a good wife to you. To make up for any shortcomings—"

"Sophie," Ned interrupted in a hoarse voice.

"I'm babbling again, aren't I?"

He didn't answer. Instead, he drew the horses to a halt. They were far from the house now, stopped near a bank of snow on the outskirts of the woods. He tied off the reins and turned in the seat to face her. He looked at her for a long moment. And then he cleared his throat. "I thought you were going to end things. I thought—now that you're free—you wouldn't want—"

"What my sister said last night was rubbish, however well-intentioned. I've been waiting all day to tell you that."

"And much more besides."

Her cheeks burned. "I've embarrassed you, haven't I?"

"Embarrassed me? You knocked the sense out of me. For an instant, I didn't know where I was." His mouth hitched in the faintest half smile. "I love you, you know. So much that I've spent all day trying to reconcile myself to accepting your rejection with good grace."

He loved her.

Her heart swelled in her breast at his declaration. For the first time in her life, she feared she might actually fall into a swoon. "You really love me, Ned?" she asked softly. And then: "Wait...what rejection?"

"The one you were going to give me this evening." He reached for her, his hand coming to cradle her cheek in that way of his. He regarded her steadily, his blue gaze as solemn as it was tender. "And yes, my darling girl. I really do love you."

She blinked as tears stung her eyes. "Then you'll marry me?"

He gave a short, husky laugh. "My God, yes."

Sophie smiled. And though that smile might be a little watery, Ned didn't seem to mind. He looked at her for a moment longer, as if she were the finest thing he'd ever seen, then his head bent to hers and he kissed her.

She brought her arms to circle his neck, clinging to him as his lips moved on hers. He kissed her slowly, deeply, claiming her mouth with a thoroughness that left them both breathless. And she kissed him in return, sweetly, ever so sweetly, until he pulled back with a groan to rest his forehead against hers.

"Sophie," he said in a husky murmur.

She let her fingers run through the hair at his nape. "I like you like this. Your hair disheveled and your cravat rumpled. It's much less intimidating than how you looked in London."

He nuzzled her cheek. "And how was that?"

"Too cold. Too perfect. And far too quiet for me to know what you were thinking. That wasn't the real you."

"No. It was..." He trailed off, eyes closing as Sophie moved her lips over his in the barest whisper of a kiss.

"What?"

"Bad advice. From a book."

She drew back to look at him. "What sort of book?"

It was dark, the only light coming from the small lamp on the sleigh, but Sophie could have sworn that a flush crept into Ned's cheeks. "An etiquette book. For gentlemen.

Her brows lifted.

"I bought it at Hatchard's the day your father gave me permission to court you. Suffice to say, the advice within its pages wasn't as practical as the sort offered by your Mr. Darwin."

"Mr. Darwin doesn't write etiquette books."

"No, indeed. And yet, I suspect you've been using his teachings as a guide. Trying to adapt yourself to rapidly changing circumstances. To acclimate yourself to marrying a tradesman."

It was her turn to blush. "Perhaps in the beginning."

"And now?"

"I still think it rather sensible. The world is changing. We can't keep doing the same thing anymore, can we?"

"No. But it's not going to be easy for you, Sophie. There's much you'll have to give up. The society matrons in London—"

"I don't give a fig about them. If they want to shun me, they may do so with my good wishes. I've never sought the approval of the beau monde." She slid her hand around the back of his neck. "At the moment, I'm more concerned with the approval of your mother."

"You already have it." Ned paused before adding, "Though she's a bit out of temper with you for rejecting me this evening."

"But I didn't—"

"Never mind my mother. Look up, Sophie."

The night sky was lit with stars. They twinkled like diamonds nestled on a bed of black velvet. She inhaled a soft breath at the perfect beauty of it.

"Didn't I tell you I'd kiss you under the stars?" Ned murmured into her ear.

"That's not just any star, Ned." She urged his gaze heavenward. "That's the Christmas star."

They fell quiet for a time, both of them looking up at the star that shone so much more brightly than the others. "Well," Ned said finally, "if that isn't fortuitous for this partnership, I don't know what is."

"A partner," Sophie repeated. "Is that how you think of me?"

He made a soft sound of assent as he enfolded her back into his embrace. "Not very romantic, is it? But I don't want you to feel powerless with me. I value your intelligence and your strength. I'd rather you stood at my side than in my shadow."

She tightened her arms around his neck, blinking rapidly against another swell of tears. "I think that may be the most romantic thing you've ever said to me."

His lips brushed over her damp cheek. He held her fast for a long while, the bells on the horses' bridles the only sound in the star-studded darkness.

"Come," he said at last, his hands moving over the curve of her spine. "Let's go back to the house before you and the horses turn into icicles. There's a blazing fire in the drawing room. And your mother said something about iced gingerbread cake."

She hugged him tighter. "Yes, by all means. We still have Christmas to celebrate."

"We do." He pressed one last soft kiss to her temple. "This Christmas and all the Christmases to come."

Epilogue

Christmas Day
December, 1861

Though Emily's betrothal was effectively still a secret, Sophie had no compunction about sharing the news of her own engagement with the entire world. Her betrothal to Ned was announced to their respective families on Christmas Eve and to the rest of the guests on Christmas Day. There were a few whispers from the gentry, but among the villagers, the news was met with near unanimous approbation.

"A love match," Mrs. Lanyon said, beaming. "Just as the Queen had with her dear Prince Albert."

Mrs. Sharpe smiled. "I've never yet heard my son compared to a prince, but I cannot deny that he and Miss Appersett are well suited."

"I should say so," Mrs. Fortescue agreed. "They've been billing and cooing all morning."

Sophie tried not to blush. She'd already done enough of that for a lifetime. It seemed that everyone delighted in embarrassing the two of them.

"You've only to say the word and I'll announce your sister and Murray's betrothal," Ned said to her in a low voice. "It would shift the focus off of us, at least."

"That wouldn't be very sporting."

"Perhaps not. But all's fair in love and war, as the poets say."

Sophie gave him a look. "The poets haven't met my sister."

As if on cue, Emily approached with a few of her friends. "Show Miss Tunstall your betrothal ring, Sophie."

Sophie obliged her, extending her hand as Miss Tunstall and the other young ladies admired the diamond Ned had given her that morning. It flashed in the gaslight, almost as dazzling as the Christmas star had been the previous evening.

"Oh, look at it!" the ladies exclaimed. "How utterly divine!"

Ned stood beside her, one hand resting at the small of her back. When the well-wishers finally dispersed, he accompanied her to the drawing room sofa. Mama was seated nearby presiding over the tea tray.

Her lips quirked as she watched them sit beside each other. She poured them each a cup of tea. "It will only get worse. People love nothing better than teasing a newly engaged couple."

"I don't mind it," Sophie lied.

Ned was tactfully silent.

She slipped her hand into his. His fingers closed over hers, returning her clasp with a masculine strength tempered by heartbreaking gentleness. "Have you had a happy Christmas, Mama?"

"I have two daughters engaged to two very worthy—and very wealthy—gentlemen. What mother could ask for more?" She smiled fondly at Sophie. "Didn't I tell you it would all come right in the end?"

"You did." Sophie's eyes found Ned's. "And it's ended very happily, hasn't it?"

Ned brought her hand to his lips and pressed a lingering kiss to her knuckles. "I couldn't be happier. But this isn't the end, my love. Far from it."

Her heart fluttered. "You're right. It's only the beginning."

"A toast," Papa bellowed from his place by the drawing room fireplace. "To the happy couple."

The guests lifted their glasses. "To the happy couple!"

"And to their future!" Mr. Sharpe said.

Sophie smiled at Ned as she raised her teacup. "To the future," she echoed. "May it be bright and full of wonder."

"It will be," Ned promised. "For all of us."

And it was.

Author's Note

A Holiday by Gaslight was inspired by the social, scientific, and technological advances of the mid-19th century. Like us, the Victorians were faced with a rapidly changing world. Many wanted to cling to the status quo, but some—like Sophie's father—embraced the change to the point of folly. Having his country house fitted for gas is just one example. In the mid-Victorian era, the cost of such an endeavor would have been equal to about $100,000.00 in the present day. So, no small sum.

Another prominent theme in *A Holiday by Gaslight* is adaptation to changing circumstances. Charles Darwin's then controversial book *On the Origin of Species* was published in November of 1859. Sophie uses Darwin's theories as a starting point for embracing a future that is largely out of her control. This culminates in her engagement to Ned, a gentleman who is not of her class.

Speaking of class, those of you who are Elizabeth Gaskell fans may have noticed the subtle allusions to Gaskell's 1855 novel *North and South*. Like John Thornton, Ned Sharpe is a stern tradesman with a strong—and rather severe—mother.

He also makes the mistake of referring to Sophie as "a beautiful creature." There are other *North and South* breadcrumbs in the text if you care to look for them.

Finally, like all my books, *A Holiday by Gaslight* is sprinkled with actual historical events and Victoriana. For example, in June of 1861, Prince Albert really did preside over the opening of the New Horticultural Gardens at South Kensington. And then, in December of that same year, he tragically passed away.

If you'd like to learn more about the Victorian fashions, holiday traditions, or any of the people, places, and events which feature in my novels, please visit the blog portion of my author website at MimiMatthews.com.

Acknowledgments

During the writing of this novella, one of my Siamese cats passed away quite suddenly. His name was Christmas Marzipan, but we called him Zippy. He was only ten years old and was the kindest, smartest, sweetest cat you could ever meet. After his loss, finishing this story was really hard. That's why I'm extra grateful to everyone who supported and encouraged me along the way.

I owe tremendous thanks to Flora, Lauren, and Lena for reading early drafts of this story and providing such helpful feedback. Thanks also go to my wonderful editor, Deb Nemeth, who never fails to make my books better. And to my kind and very generous parents who always help me when things get overwhelming.

Finally, I want to thank all of you—my readers—for your continued support. I wish you and your families (both human and animal) a very Merry Christmas and a Happy New Year.

About the Author

Mimi Matthews writes both historical non-fiction and traditional historical romances set in Victorian England. Her articles on nineteenth century history have been published on various academic and history sites, including the Victorian Web and the Journal of Victorian Culture, and are also syndicated weekly at BUST Magazine. In her other life, Mimi is an attorney. She resides in California with her family, which includes an Andalusian dressage horse, two Shelties, and two Siamese cats.

To learn more, please visit

WWW.MIMIMATTHEWS.COM

Other Titles by
MIMI MATTHEWS

NON-FICTION

The Pug Who Bit Napoleon
Animal Tales of the 18th and 19th Centuries

A Victorian Lady's Guide to Fashion and Beauty

FICTION

The Lost Letter
A Victorian Romance

The Viscount and the Vicar's Daughter
A Victorian Romance

The Matrimonial Advertisement
Parish Orphans of Devon, Book 1

A Modest Independence
Parish Orphans of Devon, Book 2

Made in the USA
Middletown, DE
26 November 2024